Some Further Little-Known Adventures of Sherlock Holmes

Arthur Hall

Paperback ISBN 978-1-78705-576-6
ePub ISBN 978-1-78705-577-3
PDF ISBN 978-1-78705-578-0

MX Publishing
335 Princess Park Manor, Royal Drive,
London, N11 3GX
www.mxpublishing.com
Cover design by Brian Belanger

Arthur Hall was born in Aston, Birmingham, UK, in 1944. His interest in writing began during his schooldays and served, along with a love of fictional adventure and suspense publications, as an escape from unpleasant realities.

Years later, his first novel 'Sole Contact' was an espionage story about an ultra-secret government department known as 'Sector Three' and has been followed, to date, by four sequels. A fifth, entitled 'The Suicide Chase', is currently in the closing stages of preparation.

Other works include 'rediscovered' cases from the files of Sherlock Holmes, two collections of bizarre short stories and two novels about an adventurer called 'Bernard Kramer', as well as contributions to several anthologies, notably 'The MX Book of New Sherlock Holmes Stories'.

His only ambition, apart from being published more widely, is to attend the premier of a film based on one of his novels, ideally at The Odeon, Leicester Square, London.

He lives in the West Midlands, United Kingdom, where he often walks other people's dogs as he attempts to formulate new plots.

By the same author:

Contents

The Incident of the Absent Thieves

Now that my Watson has left me to become entangled in the coils of marriage, I find myself, especially as I await a new client, with increased time at my disposal. At our last meeting my friend expressed an eagerness to transform more of my records of the problems that have been set before me and their solutions, into the dramatic episodes that have found their way into popular periodicals. Therefore, as a respite from looking down into Baker Street on a particularly dark and stormy evening, I resolved to drag out my battered tin trunk in which are consigned many accounts of past events. I chose one, a remaining few sheets of yellowed paper, from the years when I had rooms in Montague Street. By some, this account will be deemed a tragedy.

I had no Boswell then to record the circumstances and so it fell to me, for the sake of future reference and, later, my friend's ambitions, to put pen to paper.

\#

I recall this as one of the few instances in my career, when the client was already known to me. At least, I was familiar with Mrs Joan Rander and her family by reputation.

She burst into the room abruptly, hardly having been announced.

'Mr Holmes! Mr Holmes! You are my last hope. I must have your help!' she cried in a Cockney accent that I will not attempt to reproduce here. I rose and waited until my landlady had withdrawn, before indicating that my visitor should be seated.

'Take the chair nearest to the fire Mrs Rander, for the winter chill has arrived early this year, don't you think?'

My remark remained unanswered, and the lady lowered her ample form into an armchair. Her eyes darted around the room warily, before settling upon me. I had never seen her before but her appearance held no surprises, the coarseness of expression and signs of excessive pipe smoking and consumption of spirits were quite evident.

'It's my husband and son, Mr Holmes, Thomas and Jared!' she blurted out quickly.

'If they are again in the hands of the police, I can do nothing to help. Their reputation for stealing works of art is known throughout the capital. A lawyer would probably serve you better.'

'They were on a job, I cannot deny that. Pargeter's place, number 79 in Slaughterer's Lane, has paintings that Thomas has a good buyer for. But, Mr Holmes, they never came home. I've not seen hide nor hair of them for two months.'

I looked at her, critically. 'And you have not reported their absence, until now?'

'I've been to Scotland Yard, but they don't seem over-concerned about missing petty criminals, that's what one copper said. It's not unusual though, for them to steer well clear of home after a job, until the coppers have done their rounds and asked their questions. But never for as long as this, without any word at all.'

'Have you, yourself, any notion as to what could have become of them? Perhaps there was something else that they might have been planning?'

'No, there was nothing.' She squirmed in her chair, and her eyes became moist. 'Unless they have sold some goods and left me.'

'There is, I take it, no reason to think that as yet. I will, on your behalf, go to Scotland Yard to see what can be learned. I have some slight acquaintance with Inspector Lestrade, who may be able to throw some light upon the matter. No, put your purse away, my fees are on a fixed scale but would not be appropriate here. I must impress upon you that I can neither condone criminal acts, nor aid in their concealment, but if these men have simply met with accident or misfortune then I will assist if I can. Now, Madam, I will wish you good morning.'

So dismissed, she rose and left without a word of thanks, with the air of one who feels slightly insulted, and I wondered whether she realised that I had refused payment because it was likely to be in stolen money.

#

I decided to visit Slaughterer's Lane, before consulting Scotland Yard. It was a dismal street, currently deserted and devoid of traffic, on the edge of Whitechapel, one side being completely taken up with the high wall of the cemetery behind the church on the far corner. On the opposite side, the abattoir which gave the street its name had long been replaced by a row of square houses that had seen better times. Outside one of these a hooded and darkly-cloaked figure stood, apparently peering through a window. As I drew nearer it hurried away in the direction of the church. A woman I thought, from its movements, and I stood for a moment in the weak early afternoon sun until I identified

3

number 79, which Mrs Rander had given as the intended scene of the burglary.

I saw at once that the official force had been here before me. The lock, a very poor quality affair, had been easily forced and a police mechanism applied to reseal the door. A glance through the window revealed only a bare, square room with a dull wooden-tiled floor and paintings arranged around the walls in the manner of an exhibition. It seemed strange that such works which, according to Mrs Rander, were quite valuable enough to attract the attentions of experienced art thieves such as her husband and son, should be housed in such a poor district and protected by a cheap lock. I found a corner coffee house in an adjacent street and pondered my meagre discoveries as I ate a beef pie washed down with a cup of their strongest brew. Shortly after, I set out in the direction of Mile End Road until I hailed a passing hansom. I reached Scotland Yard full of questions, which I hoped Lestrade would answer. The desk sergeant gave me an uncertain look, but obliged me by sending a constable for the inspector. He appeared from one of the dull and innumerable corridors a few minutes later, and we shook hands.

'Mr Sherlock Holmes!' he exclaimed. 'I saw you last at the investigation of the Mortland Bonds scandal. As I recall, you identified the swindler just moments before I came to the same conclusion. I thought then that you have the makings of a fine officer, should you ever choose to join the force.'

This was not the way I recalled the incident, but I thought it better, in the circumstances, not to say so.

'Thank you, Inspector. I see from the newspapers that you have had many successes, since then.'

He looked out of the side of his eyes, to ensure that the desk sergeant was listening. 'Oh yes, Mr Holmes, I have my moments, as we all do, here. But come to my office, and tell me how I can help you today. Sergeant, kindly send in some tea!'

The sergeant acknowledged Lestrade's request, and I was led down a dismal passage to a small room containing a file-laden desk, two chairs and a hat-stand on which he had draped his greatcoat.

When we were settled with the desk between us and the tea brought in, I told him of Mrs Rander's visit.

'I remember the business in Slaughterer's Lane quite well,' he replied. 'A curious affair, but it really began before this. I would say about six months ago.'

'I do not recall a great deal of it. I was abroad at that time.'

'Ah,' the little detective nodded, 'then I will tell you from the beginning. You see, this was when 79 Slaughterer's Lane was first broken into. Mr and Mrs Nathanial Pargeter were enjoying a quiet evening at home when the thieves forced the front door and entered. I imagine they thought the premises to be unoccupied, for they fled when they saw the couple. Unfortunately, the damage was already done, for Mrs Pargeter had suffered for years from a weak heart and the sudden sight of two masked men brought on a fatal attack.'

'The men were masked? So it could not be said for certain that they were the Randers?'

Lestrade's bulldog-like face broke into a smile. 'Not then, Mr Holmes, but the younger Rander was heard recounting the incident a few days later, in a pub. We could prove nothing, of course, although how many more specialist

5

art thieves do we have in London as of now? Mr Pargeter, naturally, was beside himself with grief. He swore revenge on the Randers, although he never carried out his threat.'

'Does he still live in Slaughterer's Lane?' I asked.

'He stays there several times a year when he comes down from Causewell House, his home in Darlaston, in the Midlands, where he owns an ironworks. He was born in Slaughterer's Lane and kept the place out of sentimentality, I suppose, although I wouldn't have expected him to be sentimental as he is thought of as a harsh taskmaster at his factory. For some reason best known to himself, he keeps his art collection there.'

I finished my tea and replaced the cup. 'Strange indeed. From what I could see, the place does not appear well protected.'

'Now there's another curious thing,' Lestrade said. 'Not long afterwards, Mr Pargeter began to have work carried out on the house. He had men come down from his factory, and they were there for a while, in fact we had a complaint from the bakery next door about the noise, yet when we were called in about the second attempted burglary we could see no sign of any alterations.' The inspector shook his head. 'He even placed an article in *The Standard* about new additions to the paintings.'

'Curious indeed. But, the second time, nothing was stolen?'

'That's how it looked. As Mrs Rander must have told you, Mr Holmes, this was about two months ago. The strange thing is that, though we've wired Mr Pargeter several times, he hasn't replied or come down to London to have another look at the place since. I really cannot understand it.

If I owned valuable paintings, I would be very quick to ensure their safety.'

'Quite. After this second incident, did you or your men search the house?'

'There was no need,' Lestrade shrugged. 'The door leading from that room into the house was bolted from the other side, and I remember Mr Pargeter mentioning that every door in the place would be kept that way, when I interviewed him. I did, of course, try the back door in Carmody Alley, but that is fitted with a stout lock.'

'It appears then, that the thieves simply broke in, then left empty-handed?'

'They must have, since they could get no further. There was no sign that the inside door was forced.'

'Yet the valuable paintings were left untouched?'

'Curious, as I said. We could make nothing more of it.'

'Would you have any objections, Inspector, to my making a further search?'

Lestrade looked slightly bemused, then smiled and nodded. 'To see if you can go one better than the Yard, Mr Holmes?' He opened a drawer, took out a key and slid it towards me. 'You'll need this to get past the official lock we left to secure the front door. That's another thing - the lock that Mr Pargeter left could have been opened by any self-respecting burglar with a bent pin. Look if you must, but I cannot see that you will find anything.'

#

I paid off the hansom at the end of the road, as I had at the same time the morning before. To my surprise, I saw at once that the same figure peered, anxiously it seemed, into number

79. I stepped into the shadow of the cemetery wall and waited until she, with a last despairing glance, moved away. I followed the billowing cloak and concealing hood to the end of the road, where it disappeared into St Thaddeus' Church. After a moment I entered also, into an echoing cavernous expanse of semi-darkness.

No service was in progress. Near the altar, the vicar consoled an elderly couple. Here and there, scattered among the rows of pews, worshippers prayed silently. The woman I had followed kneeled, clutching a Bible from the shelf before her. I heard her sobbing softly.

After a while she rose, and I left the church. I waited on the path near a weather-worn stone angel, until she appeared.

'Good morning,' I said as I accosted her. 'Pray be kind enough to allow me a few minutes of your time.'

Her eyes settled on me in a nervous stare, and I saw beneath the hood for the first time. Probably she was once a pretty girl, but now her face was clouded with worry and pinched from the cold. That she was underfed was obvious, and she trembled violently.

'Who are you, sir?'

'My name is Sherlock Holmes.' I gestured towards Slaughterer's Lane with a sweep of my arm. 'I am curious as to why you are interested in number 79.'

Fear came into her face. 'You are mistaken, sir. I was looking into the bakery next door, to see if they would give me some scraps.'

'Come, come, now. I saw you yesterday also. I am interested in that house myself, and in the fate of the two men who attempted a robbery there.'

Her expression changed abruptly to one of surprise that I should know of this, and then settled into resignation. 'Perhaps you may succeed where others have not, and I will know the truth.'

'I promise to do my utmost. But what is your part in this?'

'I am...' tears filled her eyes, and she fought to keep from crying. 'I am engaged to Jared Rander. I am Miss Elizabeth Farrell.'

'Well, Miss Farrell,' I took out my pocket watch. 'I see that it is almost time for an early lunch. Perhaps you would do me the honour of joining me, and we can talk further.'

She gave me a long suspicious look, but in the end hunger and her need to know the fate of the man she had intended to marry triumphed over her caution.

'Thank you, sir,' she said simply.

We walked to the coffee shop of the previous day. The restorative powers of a bowl of hot soup were soon evident as colour crept into her face. We had both consumed excellent chicken pies, before she spoke.

'You are not from Scotland Yard, Mr Holmes?'

'I have said as much.' I smiled at the thought. 'I am a consulting detective, hired by the mother of the man you wish to marry. I confess to being surprised that she made no mention of you.'

Miss Farrell wiped crumbs from her mouth. 'That woman never did take to me, but her husband is different. I even worked with him and Jared.'

She stopped, as if wary of saying too much. I saw her difficulty, and reassured her.

'Have no fear. I am aware of their occupation. It is not my intention to do the work of the official force in arresting them. I wish no more than to find them.'

After a moment of consideration, she frowned and looked down at her empty plate. 'I helped in the job on that house, number 79. I was their look-out.'

'Did they tell you where they intended to go, afterwards?'

'They were not able to. The lock was easy enough, for them, and they went into the front sitting-room. We couldn't see, but they had dark lanterns and they knew from before where everything was placed. I kept watch up and down the street, but saw no one, and then I heard a door slam inside. There was a cry, I thought from Jared, and then silence. No other sound came for a few minutes and I got worried and looked in. I called his name but there was no longer anyone there. I became frightened but I waited until I saw a constable approach. While he was still some distance away I left in the opposite direction.'

You did not actually enter the room?'

She shook her head. 'I leaned into the doorway, nothing more.'

'And, as far as you know, neither man has been seen since?'

'Jared had arranged to meet me the next day, said he'd take me out for a meal, like now, he did. I waited for an hour but there was no sign of him. After that, I thought I'd hear from him as soon as he was able, but I never did. It's been two months now, and all I can do is to go back to where I last saw him. That house has become a shrine to me.'

We talked for perhaps fifteen minutes more, by which time I became convinced that she had nothing more to add of any significance. I rose to leave, ordering more coffee for her and advising her to remain in the warmth of the shop for a while. As we parted, I took the opportunity to slip a sovereign into a pocket of her cloak, unnoticed.

#

I formed several theories and discarded them during the short walk back to 79 Slaughterer's Lane. My information was insufficient. Lestrade's key released the clamp on the door, and I stepped into the sitting-room cautiously.

It was as I had seen through the window, previously. There was no furniture here, but the paintings dominated every wall. One by one, I examined them. I have no great knowledge of art, but a few of these examples I had read about. Again I asked myself: what possessed Mr Nathanial Pargeter to leave them in a house in a district such as this? Near to Whitechapel, the murky alleyways and dark streets were ridden with crime. Few places were safe in daytime, much less at night. The lack of protection too, was a mystery - Lestrade had said that a bent pin would suffice, for any self-respecting burglar.

Then I looked more closely, first at one painting and then the rest. There was something odd, and this puzzled me at first until I realised that both the frames and the canvas were new! Some attempt had been made to artificially age these works with chemicals, but I was now certain - they were substitutes.

I then began to consider why the thieves would have replaced the originals, since they had made no effort to conceal their entry to the house. I thought it best not to reason on such an unqualified assumption and locked the premises once again, while I telegraphed Mr Peter Gelder, of the art department of the British Museum, from a nearby Post Office.

I returned to the house to await his arrival. I recalled that Miss Farrell had mentioned hearing a door slam during the robbery, and so I checked the internal door and found it to be bolted from the other side. Next I rapped upon the walls at intervals seeking a hidden exit, but my only discovery was that this was a very solid house indeed. I was on my hands and knees in the centre of the room, thinking that a trapdoor might exist somewhere in the unpolished floor, when a hansom drew up outside. I went to welcome a stooped man with skin the colour of parchment, who took only moments to tell me that I had wasted his time since a child could tell that these were recent and not very well executed reproductions. He declined payment for his services and immediately boarded the waiting hansom with the air of a man who has been insulted, saying that he had already been kept from his work for too long.

I resumed my inspection of the floor. This proved fruitless until I discovered a join around the entire edge of the room, so skilfully hidden that it must surely have been the work of a master carpenter. I now knew why there was no trapdoor in the centre of the room or near the doors - the entire floor was one!

I tried again to free the internal door, but it was immovable. I left the house, relocking the police clamp, and walked past the bakery to the end of the street. Running parallel was Carmody Alley, a grimy passage along which I progressed carefully until I reached the rear of number 79. The lock here was of a much more intricate design, but I had brought my pick-lock tools with me and the door was soon opened.

I closed the door behind me and listened, as the echo of my entrance passed through the house. I stood in a short corridor, with three rooms to my right and a single door to my left. The door to the sitting room was immediately ahead, secured, like the others, by a stout bolt.

In the silence and stale air of the place I stood still, wondering how the thieves had discovered the hidden exit in the sitting-room floor and used it to escape. And where did they go, leaving Mrs Rander and Miss Elizabeth Farrell in torment? Neither woman could furnish an explanation as to why.

I drew back the bolt and opened the door to my left. It led, as I expected, down to a cellar, with steps descending into darkness. I took a lantern from a hook on the wall and lit it with a vesper, holding it high and taking the steps slowly as shadows danced around me. I left the last step to tread on a solid brick floor and was obliged to turn to my right, as this would take me directly beneath the sitting-room.

I entered through a heavy door, and an intolerable smell of decay filled the air. Possibly invading rats had died here, I thought. The lantern's meagre light did little to dispel the blackness, but I saw that a shallow channel had been dug across the cellar. It ran from where a brick had been removed from the base of one wall, to the opposite wall, where it disappeared. Also, I saw at once that there was a thickening to the walls which sealed the air in here and deadened all sound. I held the lantern higher to discover several deep vents, drilled deep into the same wall. I deferred my curiosity of these, in favour of further exploration, holding the lantern higher still in order to examine the ceiling.

Again, the brickwork had been fortified with a kind of padding. Close beneath it was a mechanism of springs and weights, and in a moment I realised that I was looking at an oubliette, a device that I had read was employed in mediaeval French castles and elsewhere. This was confirmed by the metal axis across the ceiling, on which the entire floor had pivoted like a child's seesaw, and by the polish that glinted in the lantern-light having formerly been uppermost as the floor of the sitting-room. This movement, I saw, would have occurred but once, and then the reversed floor would have been securely locked into place after tipping the occupants above into the abyss.

I moved the lantern again, its glow now illuminating a succession of vertical iron bars that divided the cellar. Behind these was the true horror of the place. The putrid smell was explained, and I shuddered at this discovery. Two partially decomposed bodies lay with arms outstretched between the bars, clawing at something beyond their reach. They were without question a man and a boy, Thomas Rander and his son, their faces agonised in their death throes. Bulging eyes stared at me in silent appeal, and a scuttling from a corner told me that rats had already fed here.

I turned back and found the stairs. My shadow was cast darkly upon the wall again as I climbed, and disappointment at my failure to interpret the facts and signs in this tragic affair weighed heavily upon me. I locked the house and left Carmody Alley, for there was nothing more to be learned here. After five minutes of brisk walking I hailed a hansom and journeyed to Montague Street in deep thought. By the time I was settled in my lodgings I had attained a new perspective, and a final confirmation would complete my case.

#

Early next day I requested the driver of my hired cab to stop briefly, in order to send telegrams to Lestrade explaining my progress, and Mr Nathanial Pargeter announcing my intended arrival. I caught the early train to the Midlands from Euston with minutes to spare, and commenced a few hours of mesmerised observation through the compartment window as the evidence of a dying summer paraded before me. Skeletal trees amid carpets of shed golden leaves alternated with dulled and muddy fields. The smoke-grimed buildings and chimneys of towns large and small flashed past with hypnotic effect, so that I awoke from a peaceful doze as the train approached Darlaston Station.

No trap awaited me as I left the platform, but I was fortunate enough to be able to hire one for the morning and, after obtaining directions, I set off down lanes that had until recently boasted carpets of fragrant blooms.

Causewell House was but a mile or two distant. I reached the house in the early afternoon, an unimposing structure that had once extended to a wing that now stood in ruins. I led the horse to a stone trough not far from the perimeter of the grounds, near topiary that had been sculpted into fantastical shapes.

A grim manservant answered the door to tell me that Mr Pargeter was not at home, but when I sent a scrap of paper with the words "all at Slaughterer's Lane has been discovered" written upon it, he quickly appeared in the doorway. He was much as I had imagined, a squat, blunt man with a full handlebar moustache and a brusque manner.

'My name is Sherlock Holmes,' I announced. 'Did you not receive my telegram, Mr Pargeter?'

'I did, Mr Holmes, and did you not receive my reply forbidding you to come?'

'I regret that I did not, since I had already left, but it would have made little difference. You will already know what we have to discuss.'

I received a long appraising look. Finally, he seemed to make up his mind.

'Very well,' he said reluctantly. 'You may enter.'

With that he led me into a dusty room, probable evidence I thought, of his wife's demise, containing little more than a dining table and chairs. The fire was unlit and he offered no refreshment, but my spirits leapt as I saw the last obstacle to the completion of my case swept away: along the walls were the paintings, the originals that had hung in the house in Slaughterer's Lane!

'There is a fox,' he explained as he saw that I had noticed a long-barrelled rifle near an open window at the end of the room. 'I keep geese and chickens at the back of the house, you see.'

16

I nodded, as we sat down with the dining table between us.

'What is it then, that I am accused of?' he asked gruffly.

'I am here to tell you that your trap has been sprung successfully.'

'Trap? What is this you say? I am an honourable man from an honourable family. No less so than the nobility. I was born in that house in Slaughterer's Lane, and have worked hard to advance myself. Your suggestion of anything less is scandalous, sir!'

'I will relate to you your actions since the death of your wife, towards revenging yourself upon the thieves who broke into your premises. Pray feel free to correct any errors in my deductions, although I am quite certain that the essence of my understanding is correct.'

For the first time, his expression became troubled. He looked into my face, a valiant attempt but he could not meet my eyes. Some seconds passed before he fixed his gaze upon the dusty table-top and spoke in a whisper.

'Very well, then. Tell your story.'

'After your wife's unfortunate death,' I began, 'you swore revenge on the intruders who had caused it by their sudden appearance and intention to steal your art collection.'

'I recognised them. The newspapers had carried their photographs before. They were already infamous.'

'Quite. Am I correct in my assumption that you kept your art collection in Slaughterer's Lane, not only because of a sentimental attachment to that address, but for the ease of obtaining further pictures from the London dealers?'

'It was my wife who loved art. She looked upon my London home as her personal gallery. It was harmless, and gave her pleasure.'

I shifted in my chair. 'After her death the burglars, the father and son Rander, disappeared, in order to evade the law, but you resolved to entice them into a second attempt to rob you. You removed the old masters and precious seascapes to where I see them on the wall behind you, after first having them copied by an artist, or artists. The reproductions were then installed at Slaughterer's Lane.'

'There is no crime in protecting one's property against thieves.'

'Indeed there is not, but these copies were a lure, as was the addition of other paintings as reported, possibly fictitiously, in the newspapers. Knowing that these additional prizes would prove even more irresistible, you ensured that entry to the house was made simple. Such an uncomplicated lock would prove but a small obstacle, to professionals. You then ensured, by means of bolts, that progress beyond the sitting room was impossible. When the robbers arrived they could not, in any case, have avoided the trap, which workmen from your ironworks had constructed along with other alterations to the cellar, and so they fell through the revolving floor into the cage.'

'The law failed to imprison them, but I succeeded.' Mr Pargeter confirmed in a dull voice.

'If you had but handed them over to Scotland Yard!' I exclaimed. 'Then no crime would have been committed. Up to that point, you were not reprehensible!'

He gritted his teeth. 'I wanted them to suffer, as did my wife and as I have suffered. I wanted their souls to go straight to hell!'

'And, indeed, they must have felt hell in some of the pangs of that torturous place. Imagine their feelings as, in total darkness, they hungered and became increasingly thirsty. But even then they had yet to experience the torment that you had arranged. How long was it, before they heard the trickle of running water as it passed from the drains along the newly-dug channel a few feet from their imprisonment? How must they have longed for food, as the aroma from the bakery surrounded them from the vents which you had caused to be drilled in the wall? It is easy to see why you have not responded to enquiries from the official force, requests to travel again to London, since it suited your purpose to let your prisoners die slowly, painfully and alone. I tell you sir, that you have brought into being a torture chamber, such as the law does not allow.'

Mr Pargeter was silent for a while. I sat watching as an array of expressions crossed his face.

'I suppose you have informed Scotland Yard?' he said at last.

'I despatched a wire to Inspector Lestrade, at the same time as the telegram to you.'

'Then why did you come here, Mr Holmes?'

'Because, despite your actions, I am not without sympathy for your situation. For a man to lose his wife in such circumstances is no small thing, the resulting heartbreak was quite undeserved.'

'Yet you have been instrumental in exposing me.'

'I must always champion the law. The one service I could perform for you however, was to warn you, so that you could prepare your legal defence. This will give you the best chance to obtain a lighter sentence for I am aware, as the court will hopefully be, that you were driven by your own pain, rather than criminal intent. I do not think, in the normal course of things, that you would have acted thus.'

#

I left the house, to which I had brought nothing but sadness and despair, shortly afterwards. The horse seemed restless and anxious to be away from that place, and trotted eagerly as I took up the reins.

We were still within the grounds when I heard a single rifle shot, and a remark of Mr Pargeter's came back to me: I am an honourable man from an honourable family.

The fox, I thought, was safe now.

The Adventure of The Ten Tall Men

A RECENTLY DISCOVERED EXTRACT FROM THE
REMINISCENCES OF JOHN H. WATSON, M.D., LATE
OF THE ARMY MEDICAL DEPARTMENT.

On examining my private papers, I find recorded a singular
occurrence that befell Sherlock Holmes and myself, during
the closing days of March of 1896.

My friend and I sat before a roaring fire in our Baker
Street sitting room, he in his mouse-coloured dressing gown
maintaining a black mood that had possessed him for the
better part of the last three days. On the table, his breakfast
lay untouched.

'Do you wonder that I once resorted to cocaine,
Watson,' he said bleakly, 'if all I have to occupy my mind
are trivialities such as these.'

I glanced at the pile of discarded newsprint surrounding
his chair. 'You have put some of the most notorious
criminals in London behind bars, but others will appear. You
must exercise a little patience, Holmes.'

'My trifling interferences have contributed,' he agreed
with a shrug, 'to making the streets of the capital safe. But
what has happened now, Watson? Have we reached the end?
Is crime declining to the extent where Scotland Yard can

manage without ever requiring my assistance? Am I on the brink of obsolescence? The notion is intolerable.'

We discussed briefly some past cases on which I had accompanied him, I hoping that the recollections would lift his mood. Then Holmes became still and held up a restraining finger, inclining his head to catch the muted sounds of the early morning traffic through the closed window.

'A carriage has halted outside,' he said, 'and if I am not mistaken, a lady has alighted. She stands on the pavement, hesitating and wondering if she should ring our bell.'

I knew that Holmes' sharp ears would have distinguished the footsteps from those of a man. His expression lightened, and he rubbed his hands together in anticipation of a new client bringing him a problem to relieve his boredom. He disappeared quickly into his room, to emerge moments later dressed in his morning-coat. His expression was all eagerness, as he sank back into his chair.

At last came the clang of the bell, and we heard Mrs Hudson answer the door and admit our visitor. In a moment she showed in a middle-aged lady of ample proportions, wearing a rather shabby riding-coat.

We rose at once.

'Pray come and sit near the fire,' said my friend, 'for I see that the cold morning air has chilled your hands and face. Take a few moments to compose yourself. I am Sherlock

Holmes, and this is my friend and associate Dr Watson, before whom you may speak as freely as you would to me.'

Mrs Hudson served hot tea which brought some colour to our visitor's face. She replaced her cup and looked at Holmes and myself with uncertainty.

'Place your thoughts in order as best you can,' suggested Holmes in his accustomed fashion, 'not leaving out the smallest detail. Then relate to us the sequence of events that has brought you to us. There is no need to hurry.'

'Thank you, sirs,' she said a little nervously. 'My name is Mrs Eliza Fanshawe and I reside in Kent, in the village of Tarnfields, not far from Deal.'

'I believe I have heard of it. What is amiss there that brings you straight to Baker Street, without as much as a pause to look at our London shops?'

Mrs Fanshawe gave him a curious glance. 'Mr Holmes, I have heard that your insight is remarkable, but how did you know that I came here directly?'

Holmes smiled, enjoying the mystical air he sometimes created. 'When I see from my window that your cab, by its number, is one that invariably picks up fares outside Waterloo Station, and I know that the train from Deal arrived no more than fifteen minutes ago, it does not seem very remarkable to conclude that you had little time to divert from your destination.'

'That is true. I caught the early train.'

'The remains of a second-class ticket, which sticks out of the pocket of your riding-cloak, testifies as much by its colour.'

'My riding-cloak? Doubtless its appearance told you also that I am from the country, before I spoke a word?'

'Indeed. It is a garment not often seen in the city.'

Her face cleared. 'I believe I did right to consult you.'

'Tell me then, how we can assist you.' Holmes was eager to begin. As for myself I had formed the opinion that Mrs Fanshawe was a woman of some perception, as well as of mature beauty.

'Let me say at once,' the lady said, 'that should my narrative prove to be too commonplace to engage your attention, I would quite understand. I have considered that the strangeness I feel about the affair might be imaginary, and that your viewpoint may be different.'

'Many of Mr Holmes past cases were presented to us as oddities or inconsistencies,' I observed. 'Most often they were concluded in a surprising fashion.'

'Quite so,' said my friend impatiently, 'but let Mrs Fanshawe tell us her story.'

'First I must explain how I came to live in Tarnfields.' She paused, gathering her memories. 'My husband, George Fanshawe, was a sheep farmer in Australia for many years before we knew each other. We met shortly after his return to England and married a few months later. Not long after the wedding he became ill, suffering from delusions and sometimes speaking in a strange manner.' She looked directly at me. 'You, doctor, have possibly recognised the symptoms of that strain of insanity that occasionally follows certain foreign diseases when left untreated for a prolonged period.'

I nodded, sympathetically.

'When this was diagnosed, my husband was confined to an insane asylum. He died there soon afterwards.'

Holmes and I offered our condolences, as Mrs Fanshawe wiped away tears in an effort to compose herself.

'Pray tell us, when was this?' Holmes asked softly.

'It has not yet been a year. I mention these events only because some of my neighbours in whom I have confided seem to believe that I have inherited the condition.'

'That cannot be so, surely.' Holmes retorted. 'Am I correct, Watson?'

'Perfectly. I know of no case anywhere that suggests it.' But it was easy to imagine how the inhabitants of a country village would shun this woman. In many such places, diseases of the mind were still looked upon with fear and superstition.

'I wanted to tell you this myself,' Mrs Fanshawe continued, 'rather than for you to hear it in Tarnfields, should you decide to help me. You cannot imagine, gentlemen, the sadness of seeing my neighbours cross the street to avoid speaking to me. Their embarrassment causes me great pain.'

'Both the doctor and I are no strangers to ignorance,' Holmes assured her, 'or foolishness. But what is it that has caused all this?'

Our visitor appeared to have conquered her distress. She drew herself up straighter in her chair, determined to tell her tale to the end.

'When my husband and I decided to make our home in Tarnfields, we searched unsuccessfully for accommodation. Eventually we rented rooms as a temporary measure, but as it turned out I am still there to this day. I live above the local ironmonger's shop. I should explain that the Old Deal Road passes the building on its way through Tarnfields, and it is there that most of the shops and local businesses are situated. Opposite my rooms stands our only tailoring establishment.'

'A larger village than I had imagined,' Holmes said thoughtfully, 'if it has its own tailor.'

'I am told that the community has grown in recent years. Since my husband's death I spend much time alone, and find myself observing the behaviour of those living and working nearby. I am frequently troubled by rheumatism, so I view life from my armchair.'

'You look down from the window overlooking the Old Deal Road?' I asked.

'Almost every day. The tailor's shop I mentioned is that of Mr Edelstein, whose clients are usually local people. Farmers are fitted for tweed suits to wear in church on Sunday, and the occasional landowner collects his morning suit. This was how the business progressed, until a succession of strange gentlemen began to arrive daily.'

Holmes raised his head like a terrier catching the scent. 'In what way were they strange?'

Mrs Fanshawe hesitated. Her eyes swept the room, taking in the gasogene, the Persian slipper full of tobacco and the jack-knife pinning Holmes' unanswered correspondence to the mantelshelf. I saw that she was still uncertain of her case.

'It was the similarity between them,' she said at last. 'At first I was struck by the appearance of a man, a little before eleven, dressed in smart morning clothes. He was very tall and stood out prominently from the locals. His top hat added to the impression of height, and both his grooming, that is, his moustache, and his bearing, made me surmise that he was an army officer, or recently had been such.'

'It sounds likely,' Holmes murmured.

'The man spent about forty minutes in Mr Edelstein's shop, before he reappeared and walked away in the direction from which he came. The incident faded from my mind, on a market day there are plenty of people to engage my interest. When darkness fell I closed the curtains.'

'The man did not reappear that day, even briefly?'

'Not at all. It was the next day, at about the same time, when I saw him again. At least, that is what I thought until I looked more closely. Something about his movements seemed different, and as he drew nearer I realised that this was another of quite similar appearance. His moustache and clothing struck me as identical to the first, and his face bore some resemblance also. His actions were the same.'

'Do you mean that this newcomer entered the tailor's shop, stayed for about the same time and then left in the manner of the previous day?' I asked.

'Exactly that.' Mrs Fanshawe confirmed. 'I thought this no more than coincidence, or perhaps that the two were related. Then the third man came, the following morning.'

Holmes leaned forward in his chair. 'Everything was again the same?'

'Had I watched from further away, I would have sworn so. As it was I saw yet a third man, and the next day a fourth! This ritual continued until there were ten, and then it ceased.'

'So you witnessed the end of it?'

She shook her head. 'No, Mr Holmes, but the following day passed without incident. After that the cycle began again with the return of the first man.'

'You are quite certain it was he?'

She nodded. 'His walk was distinctive.'

'Ten days, I believe you said, elapsed from the first man to the last. Does Mr Edelstein conduct his business on Sundays, then?'

'Never, the village is normally quiet on the Sabbath. The man who appeared on that day was the only customer. I noticed that the shutters were not raised, so that the shop seemed to have remained closed.'

'Excellent,' Holmes said approvingly.

He lapsed into silence then, for so long that Mrs Fanshawe became uneasy. She looked enquiringly at me and once made to speak, but saw the warning in my expression. I knew from of old that it was unwise to disturb Holmes' thoughts as he pursued a line of reasoning, especially at the start of a case as he strived to grasp the first fine threads.

'Tell me, Mrs Fanshawe,' he said at last, 'what is your own explanation for these curious events?'

'It had occurred to me that these men could be related to each other, because of their similarity. Perhaps each is related also to Mr Edelstein, since he is prepared to admit them on all days of the week.'

'On the face of it, that is a possibility,' Holmes said thoughtfully, 'but I think these waters are a little deeper than that. There are several points of interest here. For example, why are the tailor's visitors superficially alike? Why are they all tall, when among any group of men chosen at random you would find some short, some stout, and so on? Is their common resemblance intended to give the impression that they are the same man? What is the purpose of their visits, one at a time, day after day? All this seems an extraordinary way to purchase a new suit or suits, with the shop open even on Sundays. We appear to have a most singular situation here and I am indebted to you, Mrs Fanshawe, for bringing it to my attention. I think the good doctor and myself will visit Tarnfields tomorrow, to see what may be discovered.'

'Thank you Mr Holmes, thank you both,' she exclaimed with some relief. 'At what time may I expect you?'

'You may not expect us,' Holmes replied, then explained himself. 'We shall not visit your house, nor acknowledge you should we pass in the street. It would be better not to cause further gossip. Was it not wagging tongues that upset you sufficiently to cause you to travel to London to consult me?'

'Indeed.' Mrs Fanshawe looked full of relief and gratitude.

Holmes then turned abruptly to me.

'Watson, what am I thinking of in promising your services without first consulting you? My dear fellow, you must forgive me if I sometimes forget that you have a thriving practice to consider. You cannot simply drop everything when a new case comes along.'

But he looked at me expectantly, his eyes bright. Mrs Fanshawe wore an expression that was almost pleading.

'I have nothing on hand at present,' I said lightly, 'that my locum cannot deal with in my absence.'

***

The next morning we took the early train. Holmes spoke little during the journey, sitting in such deep thought that he might have fallen asleep. For my part I enjoyed taking in the beauty of the countryside, a pleasant change to the grime of London. Presently we approached our destination, and areas of moist earth began to appear frequently in farmer's fields and common land alike. I recognised the treacherous tarn that gave the village its name.

Outside the little country station we hired a trap, and were driven along uneven lanes bordered by hedgerows and trees. As Mrs Fanshawe had described, Tarnfields consisted of little more than a single long main street, with an inn at one end and a church at the other. In the distance I saw several great houses, presumably the homes of the local gentry. In another direction smoke rose from a cluster of smaller buildings, and Holmes identified these as the dwellings of tenants and labourers.

'It is not yet ten o'clock,' he said after consulting his pocket-watch. 'According to Mrs Fanshawe's account, these mysterious gentlemen make their appearance about eleven, which allows us the opportunity to see the tailor beforehand. From that good lady's description, I would say her window is that above the shops almost opposite.'

'Above the ironmonger's,' I remembered. But no one watched now.

'Quite. But look, Edelman's shop is empty. Let us see what we can learn there.'

We had hardly entered, when a small round Jew wearing a skullcap appeared from the back of the room. He seemed apprehensive at the sight of us, forcing a smile but constantly fingering the measuring tape that was draped around his neck.

'And how may Isaac Edelman serve you today, gentlemen?' he asked when he had greeted us. 'You wish me to dress you for the hunt, perhaps? Only yesterday, I received a consignment of particularly fine cloth that would look well on you both.'

Holmes shook his head. 'We are here to speak to you concerning several of your clients. Certain irregularities have come to light and if a scandal is to be avoided, with possible effects to your business, you must be frank with us and hold nothing back.'

The tailor's smile vanished. 'What sort of talk is this? You, sir, speak as a police official would, yet I feel that you are not of the force. Explain yourself. Who are you?'

'My name is Sherlock Holmes,' my friend answered, 'and my companion is Dr Watson. We hoped to save you the trouble of a police enquiry.'

Isaac Edelman went pale; I saw the change in him despite the meagre light of his shop. I reflected that Holmes' reputation had probably preceded him, even to this backwater of Kent.

The tailor slid his spectacles down from his forehead. He adjusted them and peered at us suspiciously.

'Yes, I have read of you. The consulting detective.'

'Then you know of my connection with Scotland Yard?'

'I do. But what can you want with a humble tailor whose clients are country folk?'

'That is not true of all of them, I think,' said Holmes. 'For example, that description would be ill-suited to the ten gentlemen of unusually similar appearance who visit you regularly.'

The tailor was silent, his eyes searching our faces.

'We have accused you of nothing,' I told him, 'but there may be grave consequences if we are forced to return to London without an explanation of these events. Suspicion has been aroused, in certain quarters.'

'I have been sworn to secrecy,' Mr Edelman said after some moments of consideration. 'However, since you represent authority I cannot see that it will do harm to speak. I am not breaking any trust, since it was also from authority that the order came.'

Holmes looked at the man with interest, inclining his head so as to miss nothing.

'Pray continue.'

'Some weeks ago I was approached by an officer of Her Majesty's Royal Rifle Corps, a Major Soames, who placed an order for ten uniforms of that regiment.'

'That will not do.' Holmes said severely. 'Regimental uniforms are made exclusively by the Depot of Military Supply. Come now, let us have the truth.'

'This is no lie, I swear it.' Mr Edelman would not be shaken. 'The Major explained that exceptionally, for special ceremonies, individual officers are permitted to obtain their attire privately. He told me no more than that but produced documents that indicated,' he bowed his head in reverence, 'that my work will be worn in the presence of Her Majesty.'

'When is this to be?'

'That was not disclosed to me, but I am to be paid almost twice my usual fee, with the cloth supplied.'

Holmes' expression sharpened. 'How many uniforms are still unfinished?'

'None of them are complete, as yet. The ten gentlemen have been measured, one by one, and the garments shaped. Because of their duties it has been arranged for each to attend briefly for fittings, one of which is due to be carried out,' Edelman produced a timepiece from his waistcoat pocket, 'in twenty minutes from now. Perhaps you would care to wait, if a meeting with one of my clients would dispel your misgivings.'

'I think not,' said Holmes, 'at least not at this stage of our enquiries. However, your work interests me. Would it be possible to see an unfinished uniform, for a moment?'

Mr Edelman drew himself up proudly. 'Of course. I think you will agree that I have not fallen short of the expectations of my profession.'

He called out an order and a young man appeared through the curtains, carrying exquisitely cut garments bearing the chalk marks of a cutter's guide.

'Most impressive, you are to be congratulated.' Holmes felt the texture of the cloth and examined the stitching. 'We will leave you now,' he said when the assistant had gone, 'but I must caution you to say nothing of our visit to your client or to any other. Much may depend upon that.'

He turned abruptly and we were back in the street before the tailor could speak. We walked among villagers going about their business, with Holmes silent and thoughtful until we reached the end of the village where a tiny branch of the Farmer's and Rural Landowner's Bank occupied a converted cottage. After this and a small market area, a Norman church of local grey stone stood before trees and open fields. We retraced our steps in silence.

'At least,' Holmes said then, 'some of the mystery is cleared up.'

'I cannot see that we have shed much light upon it.'

'Come, Watson. Surely the repeated cycle of visits suggests something to you? At the first, the ten men were measured. The remaining attendances were for various fittings as the garments took shape.'

'That occurred to me of course,' I looked away to avoid his searching glance, 'but I wondered why Mr Edelman gave no thought to the extraordinary resemblance between his clients.'

'You will recall Mrs Fanshawe's surmise that these men were of the military. That being so, we should not be surprised if each of them conforms to a soldier's height, bearing and grooming. Remember that beards and moustaches in particular must conform to army regulations, and no doubt the wearing of morning dress created the impression that these were gentlemen from old service families. Edelman must have known from the start that something was amiss, but his greed got the better of his conscience. Pah!' Holmes snorted in disgust, 'I should have seen it all before we left Baker Street.'

'So there is nothing in it, after all. Are we returning to London then, or calling on Mrs Fanshawe to tell her of our findings?'

Holmes shook his head. 'So you believe our journey here has been fruitless? I tell you that we have not yet reached the bottom of this business. Soldiers do not have special uniforms made by civilian tailors, regardless of their rank or the occasion. Doubtlessly the local newspapers have at some time carried an account in their small print of the theft of a number of bolts of cloth from the regional quartermaster's stores. But I see there is a coffee shop just here, where we can allow ourselves some brief refreshment before observing Mr Edelman's client. The sight of him may prove enlightening.'

We were about to enter the establishment when Holmes gripped my arm tightly. He steered me to the window of the nearest shop and pointed to the display within.

'That ornate chair that you see, Watson, is of the period of Louis XIV, the builder of Versailles.'

Somewhat taken aback at this interruption, I gazed with some curiosity at Holmes' reflection. 'An antique shop is always interesting, but what were you diverting my attention away from?'

He glanced carefully over his shoulder. 'I saw a man coming towards us, moving in and out of sight as he threaded his way through the clusters of village folk. That he was one of those described by Mrs Fanshawe I had no doubt, since his bearing, grooming and general appearance stood out from those surrounding him. His face is known to me, although I cannot bring to mind his name, so I could not discount that we could be equally recognisable to him. You see then, my dear fellow, the reason for my rather abrupt and startling gesture to ensure we remained unnoticed.'

'He is a safe distance away now, I think.'

Holmes peered down the street. 'He has turned a corner. I noticed the local police station was nearby when we paid off the trap, perhaps a visit there will provide some answers.'

The officer at the desk was Sergeant Wills, a burly man of good country stock who ran the little station with another of his own rank and two constables.

'We read much of you in the London papers, Mr Holmes,' he declared in his booming voice. 'Also in the entertaining accounts by the good doctor, here.'

'I am glad to hear that they are of interest to you,' said I.

'Perhaps you could be of some help with our present enquiries,' Holmes said. 'We are unfamiliar with the locality.'

The Sergeant beamed. 'Anything that will assist you, sir.'

'Capital. Firstly, is there a military establishment in the area? A barracks, perhaps?'

'None that I have ever heard of.'

'Where, then, is the nearest?'

'Up at Chatham, I should think.'

Sherlock Holmes nodded thoughtfully. 'So there have been no soldiers or army exercises near the village?'

'Not since I was a young lad.'

'And none, to your knowledge, are planned for the near future?'

'No sir,' Sergeant Wills shook his head. 'The only real military action ever in Tarnfields was at the time of the Civil War, which we learned about at school. Some of the farms and great houses hereabouts belong to retired majors and generals and the like, though.'

'Most interesting,' Holmes conceded. 'You have been of considerable help. Thank you.'

'Is that all then, sir?' Said the sergeant, looking somewhat dismayed.

'For the present. It may be that we will meet again soon.'

In the street once more, Holmes rubbed his hands together in delight. Apparently he had forgotten our intended visit to the coffee shop. 'Now there is one more call to make, at the office of the local newspaper. I will visit the Tarnfields and District Gazette, Watson, while you order something for us at the inn. Shortly after, we will need a trap to return us to the station.'

***

It was late afternoon when we arrived back at Baker Street, but Holmes went out again almost immediately. He had said little to me during the return journey, but I knew from his lightened mood that some of what to me were unconnected aspects of this affair, had already formed a pattern in his agile mind. I sat enjoying a pipe before dinner, wondering if he had perhaps gone to consult some military authority on the matter, when his steps thundered on the stairs. Moments later, he burst into the room.

'Watson!' he cried. 'I have it!'

I put aside my pipe eagerly. 'You have solved the problem of the ten tall men?'

'No,' he gasped in exasperation. 'The face! The face!'

'That of the man who we were at such pains to avoid, this morning?'

'Of course. Who else would I be pursuing?'

'I imagined that you had gone to seek advice from the military.'

A look of surprise crossed his face. 'Why would I do that, after explaining that genuine uniforms are issued only through official channels? No, the military are not involved here. I have been to Scotland Yard, but Lestrade is away.'

'I suppose there are cases he attends to without your assistance.'

'So it would seem. He is at present in Cardiff, investigating a series of murders reminiscent of those in Whitechapel, eight years ago. However, Gregson was there.'

'Was he of any help?'

'Eventually.' Holmes frowned. 'I managed to persuade him to allow me to review the official criminal files, the so-called "Rogues Gallery". After a while I identified the man whose name had until then escaped me.'

I sat up straight in my chair. 'Bravo, Holmes! Who is he?'

'His name is Peregrine Dorrimer, a jewel thief by trade. His military career came to an untimely end in India, where he was court-martialled when his dishonesty came to light. It is known that he and his gang are responsible for a number of robberies, mostly in France and Holland, and possibly two murders. Until now they have not shown their faces in this country, which accounts for their absence from my index.'

'This man was "Major Soames"?'

'He, or one of his accomplices.'

'What would such people be doing in Tarnfields?'

Holmes shrugged. 'Gregson telegraphed the manager of that little bank. The funds held there are moderate, enough for the day-to-day needs of the villagers and local farmers. When additional cash is required, it is transported from elsewhere in the county.'

'Could a robbery have been planned then, for the next such occasion?'

'I considered this, until I discovered that arrangements are made irregularly and at short notice. No, I am convinced that the key to all this lies somewhere else in that village, which is why I arranged for their local newspaper to be sent here daily. It may be some time before anything develops, so perhaps a telegram to Mrs Fanshawe will reassure her that our enquiries are continuing.'

**

Several weeks passed. I returned to my practice while Sherlock Holmes busied himself with incidents that will be remembered from my later writings as The Pirello Twins Poison Case, and The Scandalous Conduct of Mr Hector Raspindall. In spite of these, Holmes examined the Tarnfields and District Gazette on its arrival with every morning post, usually flinging the sheets to the carpet as they proved useless to him.

On a bright mid-May morning, we had scarcely finished breakfast when Mrs Hudson brought in our post. I put my own letters aside as Holmes tore open envelope after envelope with the breadknife, his face betraying disappointment with their contents. He ignored the remaining brown paper packet, which by now was familiar to us as containing the country newspaper, until he had poured himself a fresh cup of coffee and set down the pot. Before drinking he tore away the wrapper, frowning as he scanned the columns.

'Aha!' he cried suddenly. 'At last, Watson! At last!'

'You have found something about the ten tall men?' I enquired eagerly.

'In no more than a few words,' he said, his face shining, 'but it is enough.'

He passed the newspaper to me.

'But this is simply a wedding announcement, for a ceremony due to take place this coming Saturday.'

'It is to be in Tarnfields. The participants are significant, particularly the bridegroom.'

'The bride is to be Miss Sophia Pendridge,' I read, 'of St. Ives, and the bridegroom Corporal Alistair Corby-Troughton, only son of Colonel Redvers Corby-Troughton (Ret.) of Her Majesty's Royal Rifles Corps. That is surely unusual, for a marriage customarily takes place in the bride's parish.'

'Quite so. Possibly it is a long-standing family tradition to use that church. The son, of course, serves with his father's old regiment.'

'Her Majesty's Royal Rifle Corps,' I said excitedly. 'The same as the uniforms we saw in Edelman's shop.'

'Excellent, Watson,' said my friend, 'you improve constantly.'

His coffee forgotten, he stood up and left the table to rummage through the mass of files stacked across the corner shelves. Mrs Hudson had cleared away our breakfast things and I was comfortably settled in an armchair before he held up a scrap of newspaper with a cry of triumph.

'Here it is, Watson! I knew I had heard the name before.'

'That of the father, or the son?'

'The Colonel, of course. The entire case rests upon him.'

'I cannot see how.'

'It seems that the Colonel served, as a young man, in India. There he lived in married quarters with his wife and infant son until the Great Uprising, when savage tribesmen stormed the outpost. Every soul would have been murdered, had not reinforcements arrived in time.'

'A terrible experience,' I acknowledged, 'but what does it have to do with the ten tall men?'

Holmes' eyes glittered. 'When I tell you that those events had a lasting influence on the Colonel's mental state, perhaps you will begin to form the same hypothesis as myself. The savages forced an entrance and held knives to the throats of the Colonel and his wife, and unspeakable torture seemed inevitable moments before the relief column arrived. This was at the end of many months of siege, of living in the very shadow of death. Since then, and especially after his return to England, the Colonel's precautions against intruders entering his home have bordered on obsession. According to this cutting, he lives in one of the great houses near Tarnfields and the place resembles a fortress. Do you see a possible connection?'

'I confess that I do not.'

'Then imagine the predicament of thieves wishing to rob the Colonel. Finding his house impregnable, are they not likely to devise a way of approaching him or his family elsewhere, by stealth, and then to use force or threats or kidnapping?'

'Of course!' I cried. 'They mean to strike at the wedding. Men from the bridegroom's regiment will be there, and so will Dorrimer and his gang, disguised as soldiers.'

'So, we have surmised. The gang's first action must of course be to dispose of some of the genuine soldiers. That, I am sure, has already been arranged. However, the motive behind this still eludes me.'

'Nevertheless, I would think your theory fits the facts well enough to convince Gregson.'

Holmes sighed. 'Theories, and it is no more than that, are usually unconvincing to these hard-headed Scotland Yarders.'

'But if you tell him that Dorrimer is involved?'

'As I mentioned, Dorrimer is not notorious in this country. The best we could hope for would be that Gregson would make enquiries abroad, and by the time that was done it would be too late.'

'How should we proceed, then?'

Holmes leaned back in his chair to stare thoughtfully at the ceiling. 'Colonel Corby-Troughton, although originally from a rich family, led a frivolous life in his youth, his army career apart. For years he drank and gambled, until his inheritance was gone. Since his retirement he has struggled to keep his family on little more than an army pension, barely able to maintain his place in the community and living in a mortgaged manor house. So again we ask ourselves, what does this man possess that attracts the likes of Peregrine Dorrimer? At the moment I cannot imagine, but when I can answer that question, I will know how to proceed.'

***

Presently Holmes threw on his coat and went out before I set off for my practice. He had not returned by the late afternoon so, after telling Mrs Hudson that we would probably be dining late, I smoked a pipe of strong shag tobacco and picked up a volume of Old Sailor's Tales from the bookshelf.

After an absorbing first two chapters I looked up as the clock above the fireplace chimed the hour. The front door slammed loudly and I heard Holmes on the stairs before he rushed into the room.

'Halloa, Watson,' he called cheerfully as he took off his hat and coat. 'I hope you have kept Saturday free.'

'I can recall no engagements.'

'Capital! We shall attend a wedding in the delightful Kentish countryside.'

'In Tarnfields? You have discovered something, Holmes.'

'It is no credit to me, to have taken so long. The missing piece of the puzzle was there for the taking, at the Central Library and the newspaper archives in Fleet Street. I really should not have allowed myself to have become distracted with other matters. The affair at Tarnfields is almost concluded, save for the last act.'

'Saturday will see the finish of this, then?'

'Without a doubt. I see from your eager manner that you would like me to elaborate, but all I can think of at this moment is Mrs Hudson's chicken pie. I have eaten nothing since breakfast so ring the bell, like a good fellow. I fear that you, like Gregson, will have to restrain your curiosity until the wedding.'

***

He would say nothing more. Saturday found us walking again along the Old Deal Road in Tarnfields. Holmes had dressed in his grey tweed suit and ear-flapped travelling cap, and seemed in good humour with a spring in his step. Like a foxhound, he was impatient for the end of the chase.

'We will find Dorrimer and his gang at the church, Watson,' my friend remarked. 'They have no excuse for being late since they have been living quite close, in concealment, while their plans ripened.'

Without breaking my step, I looked at his serious face in astonishment. 'What an extraordinary statement! Either you have learned more than you have told me, or it is a guess.'

'I never guess,' he said. 'You know that well. How many times have I impressed upon you that to see is not enough? One must observe, if anything is to be gained.'

'Many times, I cannot deny it. What, then, have I failed to observe here?'

'Peregrine Dorrimer, in this very street.'

'At this moment?' I turned my head to look up and down the street.

'I was referring to our previous visit.'

I pondered this. 'He was attired in morning dress, the way the others of the ten were described to us. I saw him for no more than an instant, but I remember the military moustache that Mrs Fanshawe said was common to all of them.'

'Excellent. But can you recall that I have said quite often, that there are two objects of a gentleman's attire which reveal more about him than any other?'

'The knees of his trousers and his boots.'

'Watson, you surpass yourself. It was indeed Dorrimer's boots that revealed that he was living near. I saw at once that they were covered in mud of the distinctive hue that alters to a lighter colour about a mile from the centre of the village. The coating was still wet and free from marks such as a stirrup would leave, and a glance towards the inn, where passengers alight, told me that no trap or dog-cart had arrived. What else could I conclude then, but that our man walked here directly? This suggests also that the rest of the gang are not far away, since to live separately would increase the risk of discovery.'

'You astound me, Holmes,' said I, feeling not for the first time a little foolish for failing to make the same deductions. 'You always make it seem so simple. I see that the tailor's shop is closed, no doubt Mr Edelman is in attendance at the church.'

'As are most villagers in such a small community, I should think.' He noted the bolted shutters across most of the shop windows. 'Such a wedding is a major event and few local people would wish to miss it.' We were almost at the end of the village and the church was before us. 'Ah! We have arrived.'

The market area looked very different from our previous visit. Many stalls had been moved away or dismantled, increasing the open space next to the church. As Holmes had expected, most of the local people were here in the form of a good-humoured crowd that flowed back from the church steps. Among the farmers and land-workers, others who could have been shopkeepers or clerks stood together in small groups. I noticed several clusters of soldiers in the uniform of the bridegroom's regiment, near the church.

Holmes' eyes were everywhere. His head moved slowly from left to right until the entire scene was considered. I made to speak but he silenced me with a warning gesture. 'I see that Gregson received my telegram. He has brought some good men,' he said quietly.

I saw nothing but the merriment of the crowd. By now the ceremony would be over. The faint strains of organ music died away and some little time passed. Impatience began to show in the crowd, especially among those waiting to throw flowers. Several small children began to cry, and then the church doors swung open on their great iron hinges. After an expectant moment, Corporal Alistair Corby-Troughton and his bride stepped out to ringing cheers.

At once the crowd surged forward to the foot of the steps. Ten uniformed soldiers, the guard of honour, raised their swords to form an arch over the couple.

'Now, Watson, do you see? Our ten tall men,' Holmes whispered, holding his excitement in check. 'It will not be long.'

I looked at him with curiosity, as the six bridesmaids appeared out of the darkness of the doorway and the bride and groom slowly descended. An open coach with four white horses waited at the edge of the crowd, and the coachman sat ready.

Then a landau thundered in from the street, driven furiously so that the crowd scattered. It forced its way between the coach and the steps, amid screaming women and children. Both sets of horses reared, startled by the abrupt halt.

Holmes hurried forward. He had seen, as I had, the guard of honour closing around the bride and groom like a steel trap. This was not for protection, but to force the couple into the landau that waited with its door thrown open.

Corporal Corby-Troughton, confused by this unforeseen turn of events, nevertheless placed himself to shield his bride and was immediately restrained. The driver of the landau, his face concealed under the wide brim of his hat, shouted for the couple to be forced inside quickly and held, but it was already too late. Four men strode purposefully out of the crowd to hold the heads of both sets of horses, so that neither the wedding coach nor the landau could be moved.

The men posing as the guard of honour, seeing that theirs was a hopeless situation, dissolved their formation and abandoned the bride and groom. A large party advanced upon them, led by the tall flaxen-haired figure of Inspector Gregson of Scotland Yard and the local man, Sergeant Wills.

The coachman was flung to the ground, to lie still as the gang stormed both wedding coach and landau in an attempt to force an escape through the terrified crowd and converging police officers. My doctor's instinct drove me to help the unfortunate coachman, but Holmes gripped my arm before I could move.

'Quickly, Watson, your revolver.'

I carried my old service weapon in my pocket, as Holmes had instructed me before we left Baker Street. I drew it now and stood ready, seeing that one of the gang attempted to fight his way out with his sword.

'That is Dorrimer?' I asked my friend.

'Without a doubt.'

The sabre flashed as Dorrimer, his escape cut off, flailed at anyone in his path. A stout man went down screaming and a woman was cut about the face, as two genuine soldiers leapt at him to be cruelly gashed and impaled. A child narrowly missed decapitation and the blade struck the pavement in a shower of sparks.

Holmes and I stood directly in his path.

'Halt!' I cried as he gathered himself to charge at us. 'Halt, or I fire!'

Dorrimer appeared not to have heard or noticed my pistol. He rushed at us in a mad rage, his speed unchecked and the sabre whirling. I sensed Holmes' surprise at my hesitation, but a doctor is trained to safeguard life and to preserve it, and to act otherwise is not easy. Yet strong also is the inclination to protect the innocent and to set injustice aright. I felt the instinct for self-preservation that had guided me through the Afghan War return to me. The sharp report echoed back at us, and Dorrimer fell at our feet clutching his bloodied thigh as the sword spun across the flagstones.

'Well done, Watson,' said Holmes grimly. 'He will do no more harm today.'

The police officials restrained the gang with handcuffs, while transportation to the cells in the local station was arranged. Some men of the groom's regiment were trying to restore calm to the crowd. Others, led by a portly, stern-faced man who I presumed to be Colonel Corby-Troughton, were gathered around their fallen comrades. The bride, surrounded by her entourage and a small crowd of guests and relatives, wept bitterly on her husband's shoulder.

I had made the coachman as comfortable as I could, when Inspector Gregson approached to ask me to attend to Dorrimer.

'Do what you can Doctor, please,' he asked. 'He must be fit for his appointment with the hangman.'

I saw that two local physicians had arrived and were tending to the wounded. Several times a coat or sheet was draped over a prostrate body, and heads were shaken sadly. Gregson's prediction was a foregone conclusion.

Holmes finished a conversation with Sergeant Wills, and came over to us.

'It is over. The entire gang is in custody.'

'The credit is yours, Mr Holmes,' Gregson acknowledged. 'I carried out the instructions in your telegram, and it turned out as you said it would.'

Holmes looked at the dead and injured and shook his head. 'I did not anticipate all of this, Inspector. We closed in too late. The glory, if that is what it is, is entirely yours. I shall say as much to the local news reporter who I see near the coach taking notes.' He made to walk away, but turned back to us. 'When the opportunity presents itself, you might send a constable to search the church anterooms. The ten men who formed the genuine guard of honour must be nearby, probably bound and gagged unless these butchers included them in the kill.'

'No,' Gregson smiled for the first time. 'My men discovered them, in good health. They appear to have been chloroformed, or something of the sort. One or two are sore from the ropes or stiff from the confinement, but that is all. I don't understand how you came upon this, Mr Holmes, how did you know of this gang?'

Holmes took out his watch. 'There is really not much to tell, Inspector. Watson and I must be getting back to Baker Street, and I see that there is a train within the hour. When next you find yourself near do visit us, and I will relate my entire line of reasoning while we indulge ourselves with brandy and cigars.'

At that, Gregson was reluctantly content for the present. As for myself, I was determined that Holmes should be more forthcoming, so that I could make notes and perhaps add this affair to my collection of his exploits which may be published at some future time. I saw my chance at the station after our trap had departed, leaving us on the platform awaiting the train.

'I rather think Mrs Fanshawe will be interested in today's events,' I said to break into Holmes' thoughts. 'Those neighbours who thought her mad will perhaps have the grace to apologise. Will you send her a telegram?'

He peered up the track, where the train would appear at any moment. 'I hardly think that will prove necessary. The lady herself told us how speedily news spreads through the village. By now she knows as much as you or I.'

'More than I, that is certain.'

My friend sighed heavily. 'I swear that you are a match for Gregson with your exhibitions of impatience, Watson. No doubt you are eager to commit this little diversion to paper, transforming it into another sensational story when in fact it required no more than the merest application of logic. Very well, we have a few minutes to wait so I will recount my findings.'

'That would be most enlightening.'

'You will recall that the Corby-Troughton house was exceptionally well protected?'

I nodded. 'A fortress, I think you said.'

'Quite. Hence I surmised that to bring force to bear upon the Colonel would be easier, elsewhere.'

'In his house or out of it, I would expect difficulties, with a man of the colonel's sort.'

'But every man has his weak spot.'

'His son, of course?'

'Corporal Corby-Troughton,' Holmes agreed, 'is a fine soldier who will go far on his own merit. He refused to let his father use his influence or buy him a commission, in favour of making his own way by proving his worth. Hopefully, he will restore to their name the esteem that was lost long ago, during the riotous living of the Colonel's youth. The alliance with a wealthy and respectable family should prove helpful.'

'So you deduced the gang's intentions to abduct the bride and groom, in order to compel the Colonel to agree to their demands? But Holmes, the man is almost bankrupt. I believe you remarked upon it.'

'That much was confirmed by my researches at the Central Library. You see, Watson, I did not abandon this case while we were in Baker Street these last few weeks. I found no explanation, yet there had to be something to attract this gang. The Colonel's history held no clue, so I reasoned that our answer could lie with something acquired recently. Also, I kept in mind that Dorrimer's activities had until now been confined to France and Holland, and suspected some sort of connection.'

'It was to look for a recent change in the family fortunes then, that you visited Fleet Street?' I ventured.

'Indeed. That place is to events of late, what history books are to the past. Nowhere else is such an accumulation of facts from here and abroad to be found so easily. I have a slight acquaintance with the editor of one of the great dailies, who was good enough to allow me an hour in the archives.'

'But the sheer bulk of information must have been enormous. How did you find the items you searched for?'

'I had a fair idea of the nature of the articles that were relevant. Any connection with the Corby-Troughton family and their known friends and associates was the starting point, then a link with the Continent.'

'Which you found, no doubt?'

Holmes stared into the distance, where a plume of smoke had appeared and was moving slowly up the gradient. 'I scoured every issue of four periodicals for the past ten months. My first discovery was of the death by natural causes of Hans van Droken, in Amsterdam.'

'Ah, the diamond king.'

'The same. You will recall that, after spending most of his life in the South African diamond fields, he retired with his considerable fortune to his native Holland, it must be eight or nine years ago. When I read the account of his death, I knew I had found my link.'

'I see. That country was one where Dorrimer and his gang operated.'

'More to the point, a footnote mentioned a distant cousin of van Droken, living in England.'

Suddenly the reason behind this whole affair became clear to me. 'Colonel Redvers Corby-Troughton!'

'I never get your measure, Watson.' Holmes' hawk-like features broke into a smile. 'There is no way to know whether the gang had plans to rob van Droken, but in any case he died before they could strike. In accordance with his will the estate was split between a number of beneficiaries, with a single bequest to the English cousin.'

'Which is what the gang were after, the Colonel's inheritance.' I said excitedly.

'Precisely. They were prepared to go to any lengths to lay their hands on it. It seems that van Droken was repaying an old debt, possibly the Colonel had helped to finance his early prospecting expeditions. The bequest was a handsome one, which could indeed transform the Corby-Troughton's fortunes. It was the Moon of Transvaal.'

'One of the most precious gems ever discovered,' I retorted.

'And so the reason behind the masquerade and the entire sequence of events becomes clear,' Holmes said as the train pulled into the little station. 'This has, I fear, been an uninspiring case, although it presented one or two unique features. Now that I have done my best to satisfy your curiosity, let us return with all speed to London. I am glad to say that things seem to be improving there, since I have two appointments in Baker Street this evening. I trust that either or both of these will provide a more stimulating challenge.'

In describing the extraordinary experiences that it has been my good fortune to share with my friend Mr Sherlock Holmes, I fear that I have been guilty of neglecting to mention that his brother, Mycroft, occasionally passed on to us cases that subsequently proved to be of great interest. In fact, I grew to consider a communication from him to be an almost certain prelude to some new and unexpected adventure.

When Holmes was beset with the lassitude that, if it were not interrupted, inclined him towards the cocaine bottle, such a brotherly intervention was particularly welcome to us both. At such times I found it impossible to rouse him from the onset of a deepening depression of the spirit, but the prospect of a new problem or a new client invariably acted as an instant restorative.

I recall one bright autumn morning when we were faced with such circumstances. Holmes was at the beginning of the perilous slope that led to his darkest moods, and as I finished my breakfast I searched my mind for a distraction. I saw that his meal was untouched.

'Holmes, these kippers are delicious.'

He gave me a disinterested glance. 'Are they, Watson? You can have mine if you are still hungry. As for me, I have no appetite.'

'But you must eat something.'

His eyes flashed with impatience and I readied myself for a bombardment of disparaging remarks when our landlady, Mrs Hudson, entered to place a telegram before him. Knowing the signs she quickly withdrew, and silence descended upon us.

'Will you not open it, Holmes?' I prompted after a few moments.

He raised his head to look at me gloomily. 'Doubtlessly you are hoping that this is some new affair to arrest my attention,' said he. 'There is nothing on the envelope to suggest that, so it may equally be a reminder of an unpaid bill.'

'It would not be difficult to decide the matter,' I remarked as I pushed my plate away.

With a shrug, he slit open the envelope with his unused knife. 'Mycroft wishes me to see one of his employees. '

He pushed the form across to me and I read:

The revelations of my clerk, Marius Jackman, may prove of interest to you. I trust it will be convenient if he calls at ten o'clock.   Mycroft.

'This could be something new.' I was glad to see a slight change in his expression. 'You must not despair, old fellow.'

'Perhaps the man has lost his pen, or his cat.'

'I recall that some of the cases that you have described as most satisfying, have developed from small incidents.'

Holmes nodded his head 'That is true, I suppose. But wait, my pocket-watch tells me that the time is ten minutes to ten o'clock now.' He glanced at me with disinterest. 'Pray be so good as to ring for Mrs Hudson, so that the breakfast things can be cleared away by the time our visitor arrives.'

This was quickly accomplished. At ten precisely the door-bell rang and Mr Marius Jackman was shown into our room. He was a tall young man of about twenty-five, clad in the sombre attire that clerks in government service invariably wear. He sat down with us, as we took the armchairs around the unlit fire.

'And now sir,' my friend began with a sudden lightness of expression, 'pray tell us how we can assist you.'

I noticed that Mr Jackman had no difficulty in distinguishing between Holmes and myself, as with some new clients in the past, and concluded that Mycroft must have described his brother accurately. I saw also that, although our visitor had laid down his hat and stick, he had neglected to remove his gloves.

'My superior, Mr Mycroft Holmes, has sent me to you, sir.'

'My brother has notified me in advance. I assume you have a story to tell.'

The young man shifted in his chair. 'Indeed I do. But I see that you are scrutinizing me closely, Mr Holmes. Have we perhaps, met before?'

'I think not,' my friend replied. 'It is both my habit and a necessity of my profession to observe and draw conclusions from my clients. On occasion, the results can be helpful.'

'May I ask what you have deduced from my appearance?'

'Certainly, but I fear that there is little to tell. I know already that you are a clerk in my brother's department at the Foreign Office, and I perceive that you write with your left hand although you may not always have done so.

Mr Jackman became very still, and eyed Holmes warily. 'I am at a loss to understand your reasoning, sir.'

His puzzled expression did not surprise me, for I had seen it on the faces of many before now. Sometimes I had been able to define the path of Holmes' thoughts, but this was not one of them.

'There is nothing mysterious about it,' Holmes replied with a pained smile. 'When I see that you remove your hat and hold your stick with your right hand, I naturally conclude that this is the hand you use most. However, when I observe that you do not remove your gloves I ask myself for an explanation. As the index finger of your right hand glove is empty, it is apparent that you have somehow lost the finger. You could no longer wield a pen with such a damaged hand, yet you earn your living as a clerk. Therefore, you must now use your left hand for writing, at least.'

'That is quite amazing,' said our visitor. 'Yet it is simple enough when you explain it.'

'That observation has been made more times than I can count.'

'My lost finger is the result of childhood foolishness. I picked up my father's shotgun when his back was turned. Until recently I had a glove with a false finger fitted to it, but it seems to have been mislaid. My injury is rather upsetting to me in company.'

'As much harm is done by accident as by deliberate intent,' Holmes remarked. 'A most regrettable misfortune, especially for a boy. But now sir, pray relate to us the story you mentioned.'

'Since my experience, I have pondered over it constantly,' Mr Jackman began. 'It seems to be harmless and nothing but a silly practical joke. My preoccupation must have been noticeable because on resuming my work it was not long before Mr Mycroft Holmes asked me the cause of it. I was surprised that he took the matter seriously, and immediately referred me to your good self.'

'I cannot help you until you make me conversant with the facts,' Holmes reminded him.

'Of course. A week ago I took a few days holiday in Bath. I am an amateur historian in my spare time, and I wanted to look over the Roman remains there. I took a room at a small hotel and had been there a day when one of the other guests, a man who introduced himself as Mr Peter Smith, struck up a conversation with me. We soon discovered that we had much in common and spent many hours together, touring the ruins and taking meals together. At his insistence, we shared a table for our meals in the hotel. Mr Smith was extremely friendly and companionable, but I found it strange that he would allow me to pay for nothing. Our visits to coffee-shops, a theatre on one occasion and even my hotel bill were paid for by him, to my utter astonishment. When I offered to pay my way he would have none of it, waving away my attempts.'

'And what did this most generous fellow eventually ask in return?' Holmes asked with a knowing look.

Our visitor raised his hands in a confounded gesture. 'Absolutely nothing, that is why this incident was so puzzling! In fact, what happened was the very opposite to what I had come to expect. When I made a final attempt to reimburse Mr Smith for some of the expense he merely laughed. "I'll tell you what, Marius my friend," he said just before we went our separate ways. "You come to visit me this weekend. I'll show you some more historical places and you can buy me a meal if you've a mind to, although that doesn't matter. It's just your company I desire. Like you, I am unmarried, and loneliness sometimes overcomes me."'

He paused, as if reflecting again on the situation.

'Did you agree?' I prompted.

'I did indeed,' he replied. 'for I felt obliged to. On Saturday morning I caught the early train to West Byfleet, and hired a trap at the station. Mr Smith had told me that his residence is situated close to that section of the River Wey which is a canal connecting West Byfleet to Basingstoke, and after asking directions several times I was able to find the area. I left the trap and walked along the narrow towpath, and began to wonder if I had arrived at the wrong place. I found myself confronted by a waterway long disused, stagnant and thick with algae and weed. It was a silent place, without any sound until I disturbed some birds that had nested in the clumps of vegetation at the edge of the thick brown water.

'I paused to look at my surroundings more carefully. There were houses spaced along both banks, but every one that I could see appeared derelict. I walked further, hoping to see Canal Reach, for that was the name of the house that Mr Smith had used, to be an acceptable place of residence in the midst of all this decay. I passed a number of old barges, moored at the opposite bank and already half-surrendered to the elements, before there appeared a long plot of uncultivated land with a single house at its end. As I approached the house I could already see that it was in a similar condition to the others, and that a faded sign hung awkwardly and proclaimed it to be the address I sought.'

'You saw no one,' asked Holmes, 'for all this time?'

'The entire scene was deserted, up to then. I rapped upon the door with my stick, without any response, several times. When I realised that this was futile I took the narrow path at the side of the house, in the hope that I could attract the attention of someone in the downstairs rooms or in the garden. At one point I stopped to peer into the largest of the windows, and was appalled by what I saw. There was no furniture visible, no inhabitants or anything else! The sun shone in, illuminating a room containing nothing but a broken chair, at such an angle that I could see through an open door that the next room was much the same. I confess that I was mystified for, if this were some sort of practical joke, then what purpose could it have? Mr Smith had seemed such an agreeable sort, befriending me during our brief association, that I could not believe it of him. I could see that there was nothing else to be done, so I returned to the towpath and was about to retrace my steps when I realised that I was no longer alone. Almost opposite on the other bank stood a red-roofed house that looked as if it were about to fall down, and to my surprise a woman stood at the gate of the small front garden watching me intently. She was of striking appearance, past her youth but still dark-haired and handsome, and wore a scarlet dress. I called to her but she did not reply, but produced a spy-glass from a case she carried and proceeded to watch me through it. I concluded that the unfortunate woman must be very short-sighted and raised a hand to show that I had seen her, whereupon she lowered the instrument and turned away abruptly to retreat into the house.'

I saw that Holmes' face was alight with interest, and a semblance of his old self had returned. His eyes glittered.

'Can you remember which hand you raised, in order to wave?' he enquired.

Mr Jackman paused thoughtfully, wearing a puzzled expression at such a question. 'I believe...yes, I recall clearly,' he said at last. 'I held my travelling-case in my left hand, and waved with my right.'

'You are certain?'

He hesitated. 'Quite certain. Is that significant?'

'Perhaps. What action did you take then?'

'I could see that I would learn nothing at Canal Reach,' our visitor resumed, 'so I resolved to ask questions at the house where the woman had appeared. During my approach I had seen no bridge to take me across to the opposite bank, so I knew that I would have to walk further. In fact it was almost a mile before I was able to cross. Immediately upon reaching the house I knocked upon the door then, having received no reply, hammered upon it impatiently. This brought no result and so I encircled the place, only to find it as empty as Canal Reach and with no sign of recent habitation. Finally, after peering through several windows, I retraced my steps. When I eventually came to the trap I drove back to the station and returned to London.'

'To return to work on Monday, where you eventually explained your confused demeanour to Mr Mycroft Holmes,' I finished.

'That was the conclusion of it.'

There was a moment of silence, broken only by sounds of passing vehicles in the street below.

Holmes said to our visitor: 'Pray describe Mr Peter Smith to us, as accurately and precisely as you can.'

'He is rather above average height. His hair is black, but greying at the temples. His moustache has a rather elaborate curl and his skin is dark or well-tanned. The style of his clothing is rather flamboyant than is usual, and appears well-cut. I noticed a faint foreign accent creeping into his speech when he became excited, as he did several times in the course of our historical ventures and during conversation. He explained that he spent some time abroad, in his youth.'

'Excellent. A most concise appraisal,' Holmes said approvingly. 'Is there anything else unusual about him that comes to mind?'

Mr Jackman considered, then recollected: 'I distinctly remember overhearing an exchange between Mr Smith and the receptionist at the booking-desk, shortly after I arrived. He was apparently desperate to secure a room which he subsequently did, although he mentioned to me later that he had booked in advance. Probably I have misunderstood the situation, and my referring to it has no value.'

'Much to the contrary, I consider the incident to have great significance.'

'Indeed? Your ways are a mystery to me, sir.'

'I will endeavour to clear up all that is strange from this affair, before too long. Now, Mr Jackman, is there anything more about this curious encounter and its aftermath that you wish to tell us?'

Our client sat very still, then shook his head. 'I can think of nothing further.'

'When you returned to your residence, in London, was there anything amiss?'

'Nothing. All was as before.'

Holmes rose from his chair. 'Then we will wish you good day. Be so good as to convey my compliments to my brother, and to inform him that I expect to be able to throw some light on all this in a day or two.'

Mr Jackman left us then, looking more bemused than ever. When I returned from showing him to the door, Holmes stood at the window where I joined him.

'Can you make anything of this, Watson?' he asked as we looked down to see Mr Jackman hail a hansom.

'It does seem as if Mr Jackman's original conclusion that he has been the victim of a rather pointless practical joke could be correct. Certainly, this man Smith cannot have profited from it.'

'Not financially, I agree. However, there are several points that require explanation.'

'I can see none.'

We turned from the window and resumed our seats.

'Consider,' Holmes began, 'the incident at the booking-desk. Why do you think Smith lied to Mr Jackman about having made a booking in advance?'

'It appears to have been an oversight of some sort. It may have caused some embarrassment.'

My friend smiled, perhaps at my lack of suspicion. 'No, Watson, I consider it far more likely that Smith followed Mr Jackman to the hotel, and could not have booked ahead because he did not know the destination beforehand.'

'Good heavens! Was the whole thing arranged, and not a chance meeting?'

'Undoubtedly. Next, there is the woman on the canal. Why did she need the spy-glass to see our client?'

'The lady sounds regrettably short-sighted.'

'And yet she saw him arrive, and only then went into the garden. She produced the spy-glass from a case, but not until she had drawn near.'

'The significance of that eludes me,' I confessed.

'It is simply that the spy-glass was necessary to confirm some detail. She could not approach Mr Jackman because of the body of water that lay between them, so she obtained a closer view with the instrument. What small feature could have been so important, do you think? What is unusual about our client?'

I considered for a moment. As far as I could recall, Mr Jackman had but one distinguishing mark. 'His missing finger!'

Holmes beamed. 'Excellent, Watson. I have said before that I never get your measure. His finger, indeed. If I have interpreted this situation correctly, the lack of that finger may have saved his life.'

'You understand all of this?'

'At this stage I am still uncertain, although I have arrived at a partial explanation. Another point in question, and there are probably others, is that of Mr Peter Smith himself. If I describe to you a rather dark-skinned man who speaks with a faintly foreign accent and wears clothes of an unusual cut or colour, what do you conclude?'

'That he is from outside these shores, surely. But Smith explained to Mr Jackman that his speech was influenced by time spent abroad.'

'I am inclined to believe that the truth is the exact reverse, that Smith is foreign and learned his English from time spent previously in this country. His skin colouring, mode of dress and accent strongly suggest it. The final clue of course, is his choice of assumed name, that most English of surnames – "Smith."'

'I suppose you may be right. But what is the meaning of it all? Why would an unknown foreigner befriend Mr Jackman and then play such a purposeless trick?'

'The answer to that, I am hoping, lies in the vicinity of Canal Reach. If you are free, old fellow, you may like to accompany me there after lunch.'

We caught the afternoon train as it was about to pull out of the station. This new problem had lightened Holmes' manner considerably, for he chattered uncharacteristically about varying subjects for almost the entire journey. On arrival at West Byfleet we hired a trap, as Mr Jackman has done before us, and obtained directions to the river. We turned off the road at a bridge that looked as if it had spanned the water for centuries, and descended a gradual slope. Before long the towpath grew narrow, and so Holmes tied the horse to an iron railing and we proceeded on foot.

Mr Jackman had been accurate in his description, I thought, for the water was still and choked with weed. An evil smell arose from it that reminded me of marsh-gas, and the houses lining both sides of the canal were remote from each other and, under a dull autumn sky, appeared long since abandoned.

'This waterway was once the connection between West Byfleet and Basingstoke, as Mr Jackman informed us,' Holmes remarked. 'It was used to great extent by the boatyards that flourished here. Since most of them have now ceased to trade, the area has fallen into disuse. I doubt if a single house within sight is still occupied.'

'It certainly seems so. We have seen no one.'

We walked on, passing the mouldering craft moored at intervals. Presently we came to the plot of rough land that our client had described, and then to the ruined structure that we sought.

Holmes keen eyes swept over the place as we stood in silence before it. I saw nothing but a dilapidated house, but his enthusiasm was unaffected as if it was exactly as he had expected.

'Be so good as to wait here, Watson, while I make a short inspection.'

With that he proceeded to walk around the building, producing his lens to examine the doors and window-frames. When he emerged I asked him about his findings, but he had little to say.

'There has been no one, with the exception of Mr Jackman, on the surrounding path for a considerable time. The doors and windows have not been opened for a good deal longer.' He looked across the canal. 'However, I am far more interested in the red-roofed house over there, so we will now make our way to it.'

We continued on until we came to the bridge that Mr Jackman had described to us. After crossing we passed a good many abandoned houses, some far apart and some much closer, but all in various stages of ruination.

At last we approached the one we sought, and entered through the tiny garden. Holmes again examined every side of the house with the aid of his lens after rapping on the door without response.

'Here also, there are signs that Mr Jackman was here before us,' he observed. 'However, this door at the side of the house has different footprints nearby. Also, it has been forced open recently.'

'Then here we may learn something?'

'We shall see.' Holmes turned the door-handle and braced himself to shoulder his way in, but it proved unnecessary. The door opened with a groan from hinges that were in need of oil. 'Stay where you are, Watson. Do not move!'

His sudden exclamation startled me, and I imagined for a moment that some hideous trap had been left to ensnare further entrants. As it was, my friend merely sought to ensure that we made no disturbance to the dust that lay thickly inside.

He stepped into the short corridor carefully. 'Tread only where I do, with your back to the wall.'

I complied, brushing away cobwebs as he walked slowly ahead with his eyes fixed upon the floor. When we reached the living-room he was silent until he had studied the marks in the surrounding grime.

'It is quite clear, what has taken place here,' he said then. 'Two people, a man and a woman from the shape of their footprints, entered by the side door as we did. They then came in here and the man dragged that heavy table from the centre of the room to a position near the window. He then brought over those two chairs that you see, and the lady sat at this side of the table.' He gestured at the dust-laden surface. 'Here is where she placed something, probably the spy-glass case, and that odd-shaped mark on the floor near the corner will be where the butt of a rifle rested when the weapon was propped against the wall.'

'So their intent was murder?'

'At first, at least. At some point, the woman retraced her steps to the side door and walked to the garden gate, which would have been when Mr Jackman saw her, and then returned. Afterwards, they both left the premises.'

'You have deduced all this, from the patterns in the dust?'

'It is not difficult, if you form a hypothesis of what must have occurred and then check carefully that this is confirmed by the traces that have been left. As I have explained before, confusion arises when one attempts to bend the evidence to fit a supposition.'

'What have you found?' I asked as he took an envelope from his pocket and scraped something from the floor into it.

'A small pile of ash, from a cigarette or cigar. It may tell us something.'

He spent a little more time looking around the room, then we returned to the corridor. The stairs received no more than a cursory glance, because the dust that lay thickly upon them remained in an undisturbed state.

'Back to Baker Street now, I think.' Holmes said finally, and we began the walk to return to the trap.

We arrived back to find Mrs Hudson poised to serve dinner. I ate my roast lamb with mint sauce heartily, since this afternoon's exertions had given me a healthy appetite. Holmes, as often when caught in the throes of a case, displayed little enthusiasm and hardly touched his food. The moment I laid down my knife and fork he leaped to his feet.

'I have to analyse that tobacco, Watson. You can help me, if you will, by looking through the evening editions of the dailies and reporting to me anything, particularly of foreign activity in London, that strikes you as unusual.'

'I am glad to assist,' I replied to his retreating back, 'as always.'

I scoured the news sheets, all the while aware of my friend at his workbench mixing chemicals and holding up test tubes to examine the results. After half an hour I gave up in disgust. I could find nothing of any relevance.

At almost the same instant Holmes returned to our sitting-room. 'What have you discovered, Watson?'

'Apart from the arrival in London of a group of Hungarian jugglers and the departure of a French count whose proposal of marriage to a society beauty was rejected, I can find nothing involving foreigners.'

'No matter. I would appreciate it if you would subject tomorrow's morning editions to a similar examination.'

'Certainly, but have you made any progress?'

His eyes shone with satisfaction. 'It is as I had begun to suspect. The tobacco was of an Italian mixture.'

'The woman described by Mr Jackman would have fitted that description well.'

'And so the threads begin to untangle. There is but one missing piece to the puzzle I think, for our case to be complete.'

'I confess to being confused, Holmes.'

'Not for long, old fellow, for I expect to be able to present the entire sequence of events to Lestrade, shortly. For now however, I suggest that we repair to our beds for a good night's sleep. I expect us to be busy in the morning. Good night, Watson.'

With that he turned abruptly and his bedroom door closed before I could reply. I realised then that weariness had settled upon me, and so followed his example.

Holmes was already halfway through his breakfast when I joined him next morning.

'The coffee is still warm in the pot,' was his greeting.

I made trivial conversation throughout the meal, until I realised that he was irritated by it. It was clear to me that as soon as I mentioned the affair that we were engaged upon, he would either prove reticent or overwhelm me with his enthusiasm and my enjoyment of my bacon and eggs would be ruined.

'At last!' he exclaimed as I finished my last slice of toast. I put down my empty coffee cup as Mrs Hudson appeared to clear the table.

'I see that the papers have arrived,' I remarked. 'I will begin now, if you wish.'

'Pray do so, while I consult my index.'

I took the morning editions to my armchair, while he began to turn pages and select newspaper cuttings, only to discard them moments later.

I found something of significance, soon after. 'Holmes! I have it!'

He was beside me immediately, and we stared at the picture together.

'It is you, not I, who has solved this curious affair,' he said then.

'The resemblance is very close, but Mr Jackman and this man are not identical,' I observed. 'It is not difficult to see how one could be mistaken for the other, nevertheless. We can be sure that this is indeed someone different, since we can see clearly that he has no missing fingers.'

'Watson, you excel yourself,' Holmes beamed. 'Not for the first time, I wonder which of us is the detective.'

I felt a keen embarrassment at such accolades of praise from my friend, especially twice in as many breaths. 'I am always pleased to be of some little help.'

'Stout fellow! I see that the photograph is of the recently-appointed Italian Minister of Justice, Signor Carlo Caruso, who is here on a state visit. This adds considerable weight to my theory, especially as I believe that I have discovered the true identity of Mr Peter Smith from my index. The article states that Signor Caruso will visit the National Gallery this afternoon, to view the exhibition of Italian old masters.'

'I fear that I am still a little at sea.'

Holmes snatched up his hat and coat. 'All will soon be made clear, Watson. For now I must leave you for a short while. Pray inform Mrs Hudson that we will be taking an early lunch.'

With that he was gone, and from the window I saw him hail a passing hansom. I busied myself with a perusal of the remainder of the newspapers and then with turning this affair over in my mind. I had just concluded that, while I understood some of the recent events that had surrounded us, I was unable to perceive the entire situation, when I heard the front door slam before Holmes bounded up the stairs.

'It is all arranged,' he said at once. 'I have sent telegrams to Mycroft and to Lestrade. We must be outside the National Gallery by one o'clock, to witness Signor Caruso's arrival.'

By the time he sat down I had many questions to ask, but he would not be drawn. Until our lunch was served he talked of Ancient Greek architecture and the noticeable rise of Germany as a military power, between long silences as we ate.

We finished our meal and left our rooms before Mrs Hudson could clear away. For the second time that day Holmes was quick to secure a hansom and we found ourselves in Trafalgar Square soon after.

'There seems to be a surfeit of constables,' I observed, 'and the steps of the Gallery are quite crowded with onlookers.'

'The exhibition has proved popular. Ah! I see that Lestrade is already in charge.'

We joined the little detective at the base of the steps.

'Your telegram explained that this is a matter of some urgency, Mr Holmes', he said after greeting us, 'and before I know it I have at my disposal thirty constables. Normally I would have trouble getting more than two or three. It is all most curious.'

'Such is the influence of Mycroft,' Holmes murmured to me.

'I have read that there are important talks in progress, between ourselves and the Italians,' I said to Lestrade, 'concerning some sort of alliance. Clearly, the government wishes to ensure that nothing occurs to threaten the outcome.'

'That sort of thing is far above my head, Doctor,' he replied.

Holmes' keen eyes swept the crowd, and I saw him grow suddenly tense.

'How many constables did you say, Lestrade?'

'I was allowed thirty, some of them from other divisions.'

'So you are not familiar with all of them?'

The Inspector shook his head and looked at Holmes curiously. 'Why do you ask?'

'Can you select three of their number, men that you already know, to join us here?'

'I can, but to what purpose?'

'The prevention of an assassination attempt on Signor Caruso. If you will instruct these men to obey my orders absolutely, I think I can promise that you will be arresting a criminal of some notoriety very soon.'

Lestrade stared at Holmes for what seemed to me to be a long time. I had begun to fear that the old distrust of my friend's methods had resurfaced in the inspector's mind, when he turned abruptly and walked across to the line of constables at the edge of the crowd. I heard him call three names and beckon, and the four made their way back to us.

'This is Mr Sherlock Holmes,' he explained to them. 'I want you to obey his instructions in this business as you would mine.' He turned to my friend. 'Mr Holmes, these are constables O'Rourke, Patterson and Denley. I have known them since I was myself in uniform.'

'Capital!' Holmes retorted. 'Gentlemen, there is a dangerous criminal concealed here, but I believe I can expose him. I propose to search among the crowd lining the steps until I find the man I want. When I point him out I want you to restrain him immediately, one man to each arm and one to apply handcuffs. At my signal do not hesitate, no matter who I indicate. Is that understood?'

The three assented in unison.

While Lestrade and I looked on in a rather bewildered fashion, my friend and the three officers approached the crowd. Holmes at once produced his lens and, bending at the waist, appeared to be examining the steps, one by one, as they progressed upward along the line. They had not climbed further than the waiting constables when his arm shot out suddenly. 'Good afternoon, Signor Atillio Parvetti.'

To my surprise, it was one of the other uniformed officers that he indicated. Lestrade's three men instantly fell upon him, searched him, and led him away struggling and cursing, to a waiting police wagon.

'You are sure of this, Mr Holmes?' Lestrade said rather cautiously.

'If you need confirmation, Lestrade, you have only to look in your own files at Scotland Yard. You will discover that the murders of Mr Howard Sangster, the industrialist, and Mr Thomas Vernon, the newspaper magnate, have remained unsolved until now. Atillio Parvetti is a professional assassin who has visited these shores before.'

'But how did you identify him?'

Holmes smiled. 'It was not difficult when I realised that the number of constables in attendance was actually thirty-one, rather than the thirty that you stated. Probably Parvetti's intention was to dispose of one of them to maintain the expected number, had the opportunity presented itself. Having established that, it was simply a matter of deciding which constable was an imposter, and that was simplicity itself.'

'I cannot see it,' Lestrade admitted.

'Parvetti had made some attempt to alter his physical appearance and there can be no doubt that he obtained his disguise from a costumier, but it occurred to me that he may not have considered his shoes. As I pretended to examine the steps I scrutinized carefully the footwear of each constable, until I saw a pair that were not only different from service issue, but of a foreign make. The design and pattern are quite unmistakable.'

'Here is the coach containing Signor Caruso. You have undoubtedly saved his life today, Mr Holmes.'

'Not I, Lestrade, but Doctor Watson, who threw light on the true nature of the man's plight. You need not mention me in your report, but I would be grateful if you would permit me to be present when Parvetti is questioned.'

'In the circumstances, I have no doubt that it will be in order.'

'Thank you. Watson, I will see you back at Baker Street, presently.'

With that we watched the dignified figure of Signor Caruso ascend the steps and enter the building without further incident. I returned to our rooms alone and settled myself in an armchair to read. I must have fallen asleep, and it was almost time for dinner when my friend returned in good spirits.

'Parvetti has confessed!' he announced. 'I do not see that he could lose anything by it however, since he is certain to face the hangman to pay for his previous crimes. I was able to point out his connection to at least two unsolved murders, and Lestrade agrees with my conclusions.'

'Allow me to pour you a brandy, before dinner,' I offered as he sat down.

'Thank you, Watson. I confess to feeling the beginning of hunger pangs, stimulated no doubt by the aroma of the roast chicken that Mrs Hudson is preparing.'

He was very animated at the successful conclusion of the case, but spoke only of other things. When we sat down to smoke afterwards, I could contain myself no longer.

'Holmes, will you give me a full account of this affair?'

He gave me a knowing look. 'So that you can exaggerate and over-dramatize it before committing it to your publisher? Well. Watson, you have been instrumental in bringing this case to its end, so I will tell you all. By listening to Parvetti's admissions at Scotland Yard, I was able to connect the entire chain of events.'

'Kindly delay long enough for me to retrieve my notebook.'

He nodded, drawing on his clay pipe. When I resumed my seat, he closed his eyes and began :

'This case has its true beginnings some months ago, when Signor Caruso became the Italian Minister of Justice. He had long held an ambition to bring to trial Mario Conti, the head of one of the old crime families who had, until then, evaded all retribution for his considerable wrongdoings. This was a man who had lived a life of vicious crime, and of initiating it in others. He achieved his position through ruthlessness, and maintained it with threats and bribery. Signor Caruso was the first to refuse to capitulate, and Conti was imprisoned for twenty years. He did not serve much of his sentence, however. It so happened that a minor member of a rival family was also a prisoner, and the order went out to dispose of Conti. His wife, Signora Stefano Conti, swore revenge, on both the other family and Signor Caruso. The war between the families persists to this day, and Atillio Parvetti was commissioned to accompany Signora Conti on a journey to England, where they knew Signor Caruso was soon to visit.'

'But they mistook Mr Jackman for him,' I ventured.

'Not at first. Parvetti watched government buildings in Whitehall and elsewhere systematically for weeks, and he may well have seen Signor Caruso from a distance, but when he set eyes on Mr Jackman as he would have done since Mycroft's office is close by, he became uncertain. I wondered at first why Parvetti did not murder Mr Jackman regardless, as would be a routine precaution in his profession, but neither he nor Signora Conti wished to take the unnecessary risk of drawing attention to themselves. Parvetti, remember, was already wanted by Scotland Yard for at least two previous killings. So it was then, that Parvetti became the shadow of Mr Jackman, seeking confirmation of his identity on the Signora's instructions.'

'Hence the 'accidental' meeting at the hotel in Bath, and Parvetti's pursuit of Mr Jackman's friendship.'

'Quite so. A rather inadequate photograph of Signor Caruso in their possession had proven to be of little use, and Parvetti was still undecided. Finally he devised the plan of luring Mr Jackman to a lonely spot where Signora Conti could watch him closely, and then it would be decided if he should live or die. The confrontation occurred of course, as he tried to gain entry to Canal Reach, and the spy-glass revealed that he had a missing finger. Knowing that this could not be Signor Caruso despite the close resemblance, they then left the area at once. It occurred to me to wonder why Parvetti had not come to this conclusion earlier, but you will recall that Mr Jackman was reluctant to take off his gloves and that his disfigurement was a source of some embarrassment to him. Evidently he had lost the glove containing the false finger, by the time the Signora saw him.'

'The remainder of the story is not difficult to anticipate,' I said. 'Parvetti and Signora Conti must have seen the same picture and notification of Signor Caruso's visit to the National Gallery as ourselves, and the assassination attempt was arranged as a result.'

'Indeed, Watson. The rest you know, since you were present. I do hope that Lestrade will see fit not to mention my trifling involvement in this affair in his report. To claim this as one of his successes will undoubtedly enhance his career somewhat.'

As I review my notes, I see that it was no more than a few weeks after the trial of Colonel Moran in 1894, that another extraordinary affair was placed before my friend Mr Sherlock Holmes.

There had been little to occupy Holmes in recent days, and as Christmas approached, I saw the signs of boredom that had once driven him to the cocaine bottle slowly reappearing. We were about to repair to the fireside armchairs after breakfast when his keen ears detected a coach sliding to a halt in the piled snow beneath our window. At once he dropped his newspaper and stared down into Baker Street. Instantly, and I thought a little desperately, he adopted his habit of rubbing his hands together in anticipation of a visit from a new client. A moment later the door-bell rang, and we heard Mrs Hudson descend the stairs.

After a brief discussion she returned with a gentleman of normal height, but who was made to appear taller by the high top hat he wore. His black moustache seemed to bristle as he took in first the room, and then Holmes and myself.

'Which of you is Mr Sherlock Holmes?' He asked in a rather clipped tone.

'It is I that you seek,' said my friend, before introducing me. He called to our landlady, who was closing the door as she retreated. 'Tea, please, Mrs Hudson, for our guest and ourselves.'

'Not for me,' our visitor responded as he removed his hat. 'Thank you, but I have little time.'

'Very well,' Holmes gestured to tell her to disregard his request. 'But pray sit down, my good sir, and tell us how we can be of assistance.'

'You have not seen the papers?'

'We were about to peruse the morning editions, as you arrived.'

Our visitor sighed, and lowered himself into the empty chair.

'Then what I have to say will mean nothing to you.'

Holmes looked at him carefully. 'Let us first ascertain the subject of our discussion, before we decide on our understanding of it. I know nothing of you sir, you have not yet given your name or it would have been announced as you entered. Apart from the facts that you are not long out of the army, have been roughly handled recently and suffered great distress, I can deduce little, save that you left your home rather hurriedly.'

It did not surprise me that our client showed some astonishment. Holmes' deductions always had a confusing and puzzling effect on those unaccustomed to his methods.

'How the deuce do you know these things, sir? Have I been spied upon, in addition to all else?'

'Not by us,' my friend assured him. 'All my conclusions

were based on the most casual observations, and are easily explained. Your excessively brisk manner and movements betray the fact that you have recently seen military service, as does the emblem forming the handle of your walking-cane. The discolouration around your eyes and mouth indicate that you have recently been beaten, since your general appearance does not suggest boxing or similar sporting activities. Your distress, which I presume to be the reason for consulting me, is evident from the grief in your eyes and I know you rushed out of your house because your cravat is badly askew.'

Our client bent forward in his seat, placing a hand over his eyes. 'I see that your reputation is not exaggerated, Mr Holmes. Forgive me for not introducing myself, and for my brusque manner. My name is Caine Barnett, and I referred to the newspapers because my son's death is on the front pages of them all.'

Holmes and I expressed our sympathy, and Mr Barnett nodded a grim acknowledgement.

'Suicide, I know, is deeply hurtful to those left behind,' I said after a glance at the newspaper on the side-table before me. 'I have seen it before. The pain lessens with time, but you must endure and exercise patience.'

'Suicide?' Mr Barnett fixed me with a fierce, direct stare. 'Yes, that is what the newspapers are saying.' He paused to control his rising tone. 'Gentlemen, my son, Stephen, was murdered yesterday!'

'Have you consulted Scotland Yard, with this claim?' Holmes asked.

'I have come directly from there. Inspector Lestrade has told me that the case will be fully investigated, but I am not satisfied.'

Holmes showed no surprise. 'Mr Barnett, pray take a few moments to compose yourself, and then tell us of these events from the beginning. If it is at all possible, I will do all that I can to help you.'

Mr Barnett sat with his head bowed, but when he lifted it I saw at once the emptiness in his eyes from which Holmes had deduced his loss.

'Six months has passed since I left the army,' he began. 'I had fulfilled my commission and wanted no more of the life. On returning to Essex I found my wife glad to see me, of course, but my son was strangely remote and indifferent. I soon discovered that his surly attitude sprang from an association he had recently formed. Although our conversations were sparse, I managed to drag out of him that he was spending much time in the company of one Marcus Davery, a disreputable character who is well-known on the gambling and horse-racing circuits. He is apparently quite notorious. Perhaps you have heard of him, Mr Holmes?'

The name was unknown to me, but my friend answered without hesitation. 'I have. He is the discredited son of the Marquis of Langandale. His history is colourful.'

'That does not surprise me,' Mr Barnett said. 'For Stephen came to me on returning home one evening, much disturbed and with a tale to tell of how this man had persuaded him to gamble using money he did not possess. Consequently, the house held his notes for a sum he could not possibly repay, and he sought my help.'

'Is yours a wealthy family?' I enquired.

'Not at all. I think that Davery miscalculated here, possibly because my son's groundless boasting misled him. We live on my army pension and a few small investments, and so I was quite unable to accede to Stephen's request.'

'Trapped in this way then, it was supposed that he took his own life?' Holmes ventured.

'I have no doubt that Davery seized upon this to his own advantage, to excuse his own actions. Stephen's last words to me, before he went to confront Davery, were to the effect that the incident was a deliberate ploy. He suspected that Davery and the gambling house were in league, in a scheme to defraud customers that he introduced to the tables.'

'He had proof of this?'

'That is what he told me, the last time I saw him alive.'

'But it was never brought to light?'

'I imagine, whatever its form, it was destroyed after Stephen's death. It was his intention to expose them all. The gambling house also has gone, the premises abandoned and the operators and clientele scattered.'

Holmes took on a thoughtful expression. 'So, Mr Barnett, it is your contention that your son was murdered or induced to take his own life by this man Davery, and the given reason was that he found himself inescapably trapped in debt?'

'Debt that he was certain he had not actually incurred.'

'Quite so. Did he indicate to you anything of the nature of this deception?'

'He mentioned only that he had discovered that several others had been trapped similarly.'

'Did he reveal the outcome of these incidents?'

Mr Barnett nodded, with an expression of despair. 'In every case the money was paid. The victims, or their families, wished to avoid the scandal.'

'Did you, yourself, take any action in this matter?' Holmes asked after a short silence.

'As I mentioned, I consulted Scotland Yard earlier. News of Stephen's death reached me late yesterday morning, and I confess to feeling anger before grief. I went straight round to see Davery, Stephen had mentioned often enough that he lived off Oxford Circus, to confront him. To my surprise, the fellow practically admitted his responsibility for my son's death, saying that he had become a 'dangerous liability'. He bragged that he was quite immune to the law and retribution of any kind. I threatened him and he replied that I would be sorry for doing so, and acted almost as if the whole thing were humorous. At this point I could no longer restrain myself, but my attack was repelled by Davery's manservant, who is an ex-prize fighter. Last night I went for a short walk to clear my head, and two ruffians attacked me. I gave a good account of myself but,' he indicated his discoloured eyes, 'they were too much for me.'

'I have no doubt that they found their task difficult,' Holmes murmured, 'and I imagine that Davery's claim to be beyond retribution is because, although discredited, he has powerful friends. However, we will see if he remains unscathed by the end of my enquiries. Now, Mr Barnett, is there anything more that you wish to tell us?'

'It remains only for me to say that I am greatly indebted to both you gentlemen, for undertaking to set things right on my behalf.'

'You should hear of the outcome shortly,' Holmes said. 'Pray be good enough to write down the address of Mr Marcus Davery, before you leave.'

Our visitor took the pencil and pad that I produced, and after more expressions of gratitude, he took up his hat and left us.

Holmes sat like a statue for a few moments, and then his expression changed. His eyes glittered, and I saw that he was filled with the extraordinary energy that I knew of old.

'Hand me my index if you please, Watson.'

I extracted the volume from the bookshelf, and he began turning the pages eagerly. He studied an assortment of newspaper cuttings, impatiently dismissing one after another until at last he gave a cry of triumph. 'Aha! As I said, his career has been colourful.'

'Is his notoriety as great as Mr Barnett implied?'

'Most certainly.' Holmes held the sheets up to catch the light. 'You will be astonished to hear, that this is in fact the fifth suicide that our Mr Davery has been concerned with, apart from the misery he inflicted with the gambling scheme. It appears that anyone who gets in his way chooses it voluntarily, conveniently solving his problems.'

'Clearly he has some sort of strong hold on his acquaintances. Has nothing been done, before now?'

'As we have already observed, he has powerful friends.'
'Are they powerful enough to place him above the law?'
'He is not the first to believe that it can be so, but we shall see how things turn out.'
'For how long has this been happening?'
Holmes scanned the pages with a grim expression on his face.
'He appears in my index about seven months ago, but I have no doubt that his misdeeds extend back much further. It seems that, at that time, there was some sort of indiscretion involving a Mrs Elizabeth Velner and a foreign dignitary. Davery somehow discovered and threatened to disclose this to her husband unless she paid him a substantial sum, which she did. Of course, in such situations that is never the end of the matter. After repeated demands the lady was practically penniless and would have been forced to confess everything but decided to take her own life instead, or so says the official report. Then we have Mr Andrew Byncroft, to whom Davery was heavily in debt until, again, suicide made repayment unnecessary. Next was Mr George Cornhurst, of whom we have no details other than that he threatened Davery with exposure of some past dishonesty, or worse.

Finally, Mr Benjamin Selter took his own life after discovering Davery in the act of burgling his house. An extraordinary pattern of events, wouldn't you say, Watson?'

'It is appalling,' I replied in disgust. 'What kind of man can he be, Holmes? How does he induce his victims to end their own lives?'

'Perhaps this can be determined, during the investigation.'

'Could it be Mesmerism?'

'There is no mention of Davery possessing hypnotic skills, either in the official report or elsewhere in my index. Nevertheless, at this stage we cannot rule it out. I know that you have to attend to your patients this morning, doctor, so I will visit Davery alone. If you would care to hear the outcome of this, I should be back by three.'

At that we took up our hats and coats and left Baker Street together. Outside, much of the snow had been cleared but the traffic was heavy, so that Holmes had difficulty in securing a hansom. We were about to separate when a boyish figure emerged from the passing crowds to accost us.

'Mr Sherlock Holmes and Doctor Watson, I presume?' He said with a humorous air.
'Indeed,' replied Holmes. 'And you, sir?'

'You will know of me already, for Mr Caine Barnett has consulted you this very morning. I am Marcus Davery.'

I immediately took stock of him, for he was not in the least as I expected. Dark-skinned and tall, but not of Holmes' height, and clad in a rather flamboyant morning-coat and narrow-brimmed top hat, he had an engaging smile. His eyes shone with amusement, as if he saw everything before him as some light hearted jest or schoolboy prank, and my first impression of his youth was contradicted only slightly on close inspection.

'Do you wish to discuss your dealings with my client?'

Marcus Davery laughed shortly. 'Nothing could be further from my mind, Mr Holmes. The only reason that I am spending a few minutes of my time here is to do you the service of warning you against wasting yours. You will achieve nothing, sir, with any pursuit of my affairs. What is done is past, to Mr Barnett's detriment, but to my advantage. I am a man who makes his way through life without the burdens of regret. I fear nothing, nor any man. You would do well to remember that.'

I felt my temper rising at the man's impudence, but Holmes put a hand on my arm to indicate that I should stay silent.

'This is not the first time I have heard such words from those who feel they are above the law,' he said then. 'I have been threatened often, yet here I am. However, since you had the foresight to follow Mr Barnett here, Mr Davery, I acknowledge that you are a force to be reckoned with.'

'You would do well to consider me as such. Mr Barnett threatened me and was punished for his pains. Naturally I kept track of him to determine his future intentions, and he led me to you.'

'Are you not afraid that such outrageous conduct might attract the attention of Scotland Yard?'

Marcus Davery gave a contemptuous snort. 'That place exists to keep the little men and women, the inconsequential rabble of the capital, in order. It is a protection for the ruling classes against the legions of the unwashed. No sir, I am unafraid of these blundering oafs who are employed to restrain their peers.'

'Thank you, Mr Davery,' Holmes stare was expressionless. 'You have made things very clear.'

'See that you remember my warning. Be aware that my vengeance comes from high places.'

'I assure you that I will forget nothing about you.'

Davery gave us a long cold look, and I saw that his eyes were blank like those of a mannequin and without sentiment or feeling. Abruptly he turned and walked away, swinging his cane and singing softly to himself.
'That man is criminally mad,' I said to Holmes. 'His impertinence is almost unendurable.'

To my surprise, my friend laughed. 'Your diagnosis is doubtlessly correct, doctor. But we shall see where his view of the world leaves him, in the end.' He signalled a passing hansom. 'We have met his kind before.'
We went our separate ways. It was a little after three when I returned to our rooms through a flurry of snow, but there was no sign of Holmes. I settled into an armchair to

read when the front door opened and closed noisily, and I heard his familiar tread upon the stairs.

'Ah, Watson!' he cried as he burst into the room. 'I have had a most successful day. Kindly ring for Mrs Hudson, and I will tell you all over tea.'

I had spent a mundane day at my surgery, and so was keen to hear of my friend's experiences.

'My first destination was the docks,' Holmes began presently as he pushed away his empty cup. 'In fact, I visited several harbour masters with the same request, until I found a description of a certain voyage in the records.'

'But what has this to do with Davery?' I enquired.

'You will recall that his complexion was rather dark, but not so much so as to be recently returned from the tropics. I deduced from this that he had returned from such a journey some months ago, and postulated that the suicides began since his return.'

'Did you confirm this?'

'I did so by consulting the Port of London journals that are maintained by every harbour master. Marcus Davery returned from East Africa via Mombasa, less than a month before his first victim took her own life. I knew where to look because I noticed his signet ring, which bore a design typical of the native art of that region.'

'You believe that his strange control over others originates there, then?'

'It appears likely, but we shall see. From there I went to one of those little places I keep around London, where I changed my appearance to that of an unemployed labourer. I then kept a watch on Davery's house until I was certain that he was still absent, and that the maid had left for the day. The manservant, Manners, is indeed an ex-prize fighter, as Mr Barnett surmised, but he is not such a bad fellow after all. Pretending to look for work, I engaged him in conversation and managed to learn his hours of service, those of the maid and about Davery's regular haunts and movements. I am convinced, however, that Manners knows nothing about his master's crimes or how they may have been committed. The encounter ended with him recommending another household where he thought there is work to be had.'

'You have done exceedingly well, Holmes, but I fail to see how Davery could have kept his misdeeds a secret from his manservant so successfully.'

'I imagine he would have related the facts to him, if he thought it necessary, justifying his own actions in every case. Davery strikes me as a man who covers his tracks well, but Manners seems to be a man who would leave his position rather than involve himself in anything dishonourable.'

'Did you learn anything further?'

Holmes began to stuff one of the pipes from his rack with coarse black shag.

'I did. After resuming my own appearance, my final destination was the British Museum. There I sought out Professor Egbert Faye of the department of African Studies. I discussed with him several possibilities that have occurred to me, since learning of Davery's apparent ability to confer suicide on others. As a result, I have eliminated all likely methods but one. Nevertheless, before I proceed, I must have proof that Davery actually works in this way. I propose to obtain such proof, tonight.'

'If you need me Holmes, I am with you.'

'As I knew you would be. Where would I be, without my Watson?'

#

No more snow fell that day, but when darkness approached it was accompanied by a bleak, bitter cold. I kept warm by walking up and down in front of Davery's house, beating my hands together in their thick leather gloves and watching my cloudy exhalations.

Holmes had assured me that both Davery and his manservant would be absent, and the maid also as she worked only part-time. My function was to rap upon the door at the sight of a constable or any other threat but, unsurprisingly in this weather, I had seen no one.

The front door opened, and the shadowy figure of my friend emerged. He left the house as silently as he had entered it, expertly using his pick locks, not long before. In moments he was beside me and we were striking out down the gas-lit street.

'You have said before now, that had you not been a consulting detective you might have been a successful cracksman,' I reminded him. 'That skill does not seem to have left you.'

'And glad I am of it. I have in my pocket five envelopes, each containing a possible solution to our problem. When I have analysed these, we should know much more.'

'I am relieved that you found what you sought, without leaving Davery any indication of your visit.'

Holmes laughed shortly. 'Much to the contrary, Watson. If Davery is at all astute he will quickly realise that he has been burgled, even if little has apparently been taken. I have left some small indications. It will not take him long, I think, to deduce the identity of his visitor.'

'My dear fellow!' I cried in astonishment. 'I cannot understand you placing yourself in needless danger! Is it wise to invite Davery's vengeance? Did not Mr Barnett suffer for doing so?'

'Calm yourself, doctor, and try to have patience. I intend to force Davery into a position where he can do nothing against me, despite my being a continual trial to him. I have no reason to think that this stratagem will prove difficult, but it will be as well if you continue with your practice for the time being and play no part in this.'

'If that is what you wish, but it does not sit well with me.'

'I know, old friend, but it is for the best. You will see, I promise you.'

Holmes spent most of the following day at his work bench. On returning from my practice I was greeted with a thick and pungent atmosphere, alleviated only by his cheerful announcement of success.

'I must apologise for the smell in here, Watson, but I have at least opened the window. I can now say that Davery's extraordinary power to induce suicide is a mystery no more. After testing the contents of my five envelopes, one sample stands out as a drug that dissolves the willpower. Professor Faye was right, in every respect.'

'So, it remains only to prevent Davery from committing more outrages.'

'Indeed, and I shall set out upon that course tomorrow.'

Holmes was as good as his word. His first act was to secure two prize fighters to accompany him, much larger and uglier brutes than Manners, through McMurdo, who he knew of old. The three followed Davery's every move for the next ten days, even watching his house at night. They made no effort to conceal themselves, so that their presence always hung over him. At no time were they approached, although Davery did at first fling a few sneering glances in their direction, and as things progressed Holmes was able to observe repeatedly the absolute arrogance of the man.

His treatment of his tailor, for keeping him waiting for a fitting, bordered on violence, while he actually struck his wine merchant on discovering that his favourite vintage was sold out!

My friend achieved his objective with superlative success. As he had predicted, he had become an inconvenience that Davery could do nothing about.

Then, as we repaired to our armchairs after an evening meal of Mrs Hudson's fish pie, a visitor arrived.

'Lestrade!' Holmes cried, as Mrs Hudson closed our door behind the inspector. 'Take a chair and sit with us. Watson, a brandy for the inspector.'

'No, thank you, Mr Holmes.' Lestrade brushed snow from the shoulders of his greatcoat. 'I will stand if you don't mind.'

'I perceive from your rather glum expression that you are here on official business.

'I am, and I take no pleasure in it.'

'Pray tell us then.'

I saw that the little detective was clearly embarrassed, as if he were about to deliver a message that he personally disapproved of. He stood for a moment, hat in hand, in silence.

'This afternoon I was called to see the Assistant Commissioner,' he said then. 'It seems, Mr Holmes, that you have been hounding a member of the aristocracy quite without cause. My superiors, in recognition of the help you have given us before now, have instructed me to warn you of the possible consequences, before charges can be laid.'

'Ah, we are talking of Marcus Davery,' my friend responded. 'That man has murdered several times, Lestrade, and I believe that you know that as well as I. Did he perhaps send a friend or relative who is acquainted with the Assistant Commissioner to make this request of him?'

'His cousin, Sir Godfrey Taranet'.

'To put your superior in a position where it was difficult for him to refuse, obviously. I should think that Sir Godfrey is the only member of Davery's family still in social contact with him, since he was discredited. Come, inspector, after all these years I know you well. You feel the injustice of allowing the privileged to escape the law as keenly as I.'

'I do, but what am I to say? I am caught between what I feel to be right and my orders.'

'He is trapped in an intolerable position, Holmes,' I observed.

'He is indeed,' Holmes put a paper spill into the fire and lit his pipe from it, 'and I have no wish to add to the situation. Yet I cannot, in good conscience, allow a man who I know to be guilty to escape in such circumstances.'

I nodded thoughtfully. 'A dilemma, then?'

Lestrade looked at both of us. 'I have to see the Assistant Commissioner tomorrow, with your answer.'

'You may tell him,' Holmes blew out a cloud of fragrant smoke, 'that in any case my investigation is almost complete. I do not expect it to extend beyond Christmas. Ask him, for he must feel as you and I, and he is in the same position, to turn a blind eye for the next few days. In exchange, I give my word that I will not lay a finger on Marcus Davery, at any time.'

Lestrade looked relieved. 'Thank you, Mr Holmes.'

'Now will you stay for a brandy, or perhaps a cigar?'

For the first time, the inspector smiled. 'I regret that I cannot. From here I go to look into a disturbance in Whitechapel.'

'Goodnight then, inspector.'

Lestrade turned and made for the door. Before he reached it he stopped and faced us again. 'Merry Christmas, gentlemen!'

Before we could reply, he had gone out into the snow.

#

For four days more, Holmes continued his observation of Marcus Davery. It was after that, by the early post on Christmas morning, that the letter arrived.

'A message from Davery,' my friend explained. 'He is of stronger stock than I thought, for I had expected something from him before this.'

'He knows now that his attempt to use Scotland Yard against you was not wholly successful,' said I.

'Undoubtedly. He suggests a meeting, tomorrow afternoon at the Agora Club, to set things straight between us. His language is exceedingly polite.'

'The Agora Club? I cannot say that I know it.'

'It is in Pall Mall, at the opposite end to the Diogenes Club, but very different. A meeting-place for political discussion with, I hear, its fair share of lunatics and fanatics. I thought it had closed temporarily, for repairs to its inner structure,'

'So, the building will be deserted? This is a trap, Holmes.'

'Oh, I am quite sure of that,' my friend agreed, 'but who will fall into it has yet to be determined.'

'You cannot trust that man. To do so would be tantamount to suicide.'

'You choose your words well, Watson.'

I was obliged to visit an elderly patient, which took up most of the morning. When I returned, Holmes was dragging out a dusty old chest from his room. He opened it near one of the armchairs, where he sat while examining the contents. I saw bundles of papers marked 'Montague Street', a short crowbar, a naval officer's cap and several other small items that must have held some significance for him. Finally, he produced a pistol that was much larger than the weapons we usually carried, placed it to one side and returned the chest to whence it came.

Soon after, Mrs Hudson appeared. As befitted the season, she was full of good cheer as she served our roast duck and plum pudding. Holmes behaved like someone forced into endurance for the sake of propriety and was clearly glad when the ritual was over.

'Watson,' he said as we sat with glasses of port in our armchairs afterwards, 'I fear that I must leave you to enjoy the next glass or two of this excellent vintage, alone. However, I will be no further away than my workbench, and it will not be for long.'

With that he drained his glass and went to the far side of the room, taking with him the pistol he had found earlier. He stood thoughtfully among his chemical apparatus, then I saw him raise a hammer and strike several times. I concluded that he had decided to use this weapon against Davery, if it became necessary, and was repairing it.

The remainder of the day was spent talking of our past adventures, and in general conversation. Holmes produced a box of cigars that he had saved, so he said, for a special occasion. We finished the bottle of port, this interrupted by the wine we shared with Mrs Hudson when she brought a plate of sandwiches in the early evening. We retired early.

The next day saw me complete the responsibilities of my practice with unaccustomed haste. Holmes had mentioned that his appointment with Davery was for three o'clock, but after battling with a new snowfall I arrived back at Baker Street not long after two.

I found him ready to depart, staring from the window. 'Halloa, Watson. I trust your morning went well?'

'It was uneventful,' I told him, 'but I am more concerned about you. At least take me with you, for there is no telling what this man is capable of.'

Sherlock Holmes turned to me and smiled warmly. 'You have always been the best of friends to me, Watson. No man could have expected better. If I am going into mortal danger it is not something new to me, as you know well. I have every reason to believe that I will return here later with this affair completed and Davery unable to continue his callous ways but, in case things should take a different turn, let us shake hands now and always remember the adventures we shared. Goodbye, old friend, for however long.'

With that he turned abruptly and left, leaving me stunned and with my hand still extended. As I looked down through the swirling snow, watching Holmes board a slowly passing hansom, I was gripped by despair. The memory of his apparent demise at the Reichenbach Falls was still fresh in my memory, and his exit now after refusing my help in the face of danger, and with so little ceremony, caused my spirits to plummet.

I sat in my usual armchair for a little while with my elbows on my knees, staring at the carpet but seeing nothing but the imagined tragedy that I was convinced would shortly take place. A dark depression swept over me.

Inevitably, my thoughts strayed to the past, to the mysteries we had unravelled together. Was this to be the end, by means of a man like Davery?

Then I saw a light in the blackness! It occurred to me that I had disobeyed Holmes before, sometimes resulting in actually helping him towards success. In a moment I had put all doubt out of my mind and, pausing only to collect my service revolver and the crowbar from my friend's chest, took up my hat and coat and went out.

The inclement weather had greatly reduced the traffic. Both passers-by and horses made their way with difficulty, but a cab put down a fare across the street and I ran for it, slipping and sliding. Progress was naturally slower, through streets with indistinct white figures and the strange quality that snow gives to ordinary sounds.

It was almost a quarter past three, when I stood at last opposite the Agora Club. Pall Mall was all but deserted and I realised then that I had no means of entry, when a short man in the uniform of a waiter came out through the high double-doors and hurried away. When he was lost from my sight I crossed the street. The footprints on the steps showed clearly that the snow had been disturbed three times, by Davery, Holmes and the departing waiter, I concluded.

The doors of course, were locked. Regardless of the snow I considered forcing them, in such an exposed position, to be a last resort. The side of the building seemed a better prospect, having a narrow door which was probably a service entrance, and I used the crowbar after ensuring that I was not observed.

I was faced with a small hallway with two doors leading off, both securely bolted. Before me was a flight of curving stairs, which I ascended with great stealth. They led to a landing on the first floor, from which it was not possible to proceed further because, as Holmes had mentioned, part of the inner structure was under repair.

I peered cautiously over the thick oak bannister, into a small private room. Almost directly below was a table, set with white napkins. Holmes and Davery sat on opposite sides, facing each other, under a gas chandelier. A crystal glass stood before each man, half-filled. The waiter had fulfilled his function and departed.

'Thank you so much for coming, Mr Holmes.' Even from this distance I recognised the voice and the boyish smile that I remembered. Davery was dressed immaculately, his hat at the side of the table near that of Holmes.

'I was curious to see what it was that you believe we have to discuss.'

'Of course, it is natural that you would be. I am anxious to show you that your recent pursuit of me is without purpose. You are wrong to believe the slanderous things about me that newspapers and others are so quick to lay before the public.'

Holmes looked at him curiously. 'Have you forgotten your admissions, when you intercepted Doctor Watson and myself, in Baker Street?'

'Oh that.' Davery adopted a comic expression, like a disobedient child who tries to make light of his misdemeanours. 'There I must apologise. Mr Barnett had angered me with his accusations and put me to the inconvenience of following him in order to discover his intentions. But wait, I am being a poor host! Let us drink to misunderstandings, possible reconciliation and, of course, our Queen.'

To my amazement I saw Holmes, without the slightest hesitation, take up his glass and drink. I felt a shudder pass through me, because even with my lesser deductive powers I realised that this was undoubtedly Davery's way of administering the drug that Holmes had identified.

My conviction was strengthened by the relief that clearly showed in Davery's expression.

'Mr Holmes,' he said then, 'you really must allow for my point of view.'

'Under the law, we are all equal,' my friend reminded him. 'There can be no distinction for position, nor privilege. Are not the higher orders looked upon to set the example? But you, sir, have abused your position in life with murderous intent. Your conduct cannot be excused!'

'I have done only things which I considered necessary for my own continued welfare. You surely cannot equate the obstacles that I have removed, with the importance of that?'

I expected a sharp reply to such an outrageous statement, but Holmes was silent. I knew then that the drug had done its work.

'Well, Mr Holmes, what have you to say to that?' Davery knew the signs, and triumph entered his voice.

Holmes said nothing still. Davery walked around the table and approached him. For an instant I thought he would strike my friend, but he simply stood gloating and smiling with triumph.

'Ah, yes, this will be useful.' He took Holmes' pistol, from where it was displayed with curious prominence in the pocket of his ulster and laid it on the table before my friend.

Holmes sat unmoving, as if he were asleep, although his eyes were open.

'I know that you hear me, Holmes, because I am familiar with the properties of the compound that I instructed Gibbons, our waiter, to mix with your drink. I shall have no fears of him running to Scotland Yard when your death is discovered, since I intend to arrange a convenient accident for him before then. You are unable to move, as I am sure you have already found, except at my command. The substance responsible is used by witchdoctors in East Africa, where I observed its application during my travels. You will have realised that I have used this to remove various impediments from my life, including those you were investigating. I feel that I have been exceedingly patient in your case, since I went to the trouble of warning you through slight acquaintances in the official police.' He raised his hands and shook his head, as if in hopeless resignation. 'However, it has all come to this in the end.' He turned abruptly and resumed his place at the table.

There were a few minutes of absolute silence, save for the faint howl of the wind through the building. I let my hand fall to the pocket of my coat, to feel the reassuring presence of my service revolver, and waited.

Davery drained his glass. 'Well, I see no purpose in prolonging the matter. Stand up, Holmes, and face me.'

I watched with a curious fascination, as my friend rose obediently.

'There is a pistol on the table before you. Reach out and pick it up.'

Holmes did so.

'Put it to your head.'

Holmes did not move.

'Put it to your head.' Davery repeated. 'I command you.'

Holmes remained still.

'Do as I order,' Davery's voice was rising and although I could not see from where I stood, I knew that his eyes would now hold the emptiness that I had noticed in Baker Street. I remembered also his instability that Holmes had described witnessing.

Holmes replaced the pistol on the table and turned away.

For a moment Davery stood in amazement, then he brought his fist crashing down on the table. 'OBEY ME!'

Holmes walked stiffly, like a sleepwalker, towards the door.

'COME BACK! DO AS I SAY, THIS INSTANT!'

Holmes did not falter, but Davery was enraged. He snatched up the pistol and flung the table away from him. I drew my own weapon, but Davery had moved out of my sight. I turned and ran for the stairs, but I knew the situation was hopeless as the report filled the building. I was outside in a moment, running and sliding for the front of the building as I prayed that Holmes' wound was not fatal. I swore to myself that Davery would not leave this place alive, if he had killed my friend.

I came to an uncertain halt outside the high double-doors. I whipped out the crowbar from my pocket and was about to force my way in, when the doors opened and Holmes stepped out, alert and unscathed.

'Ah, Watson,' he said in a matter-of-fact tone. 'I was quite sure that we would meet here'.

'Holmes! What happened in there? Are you injured?

'Not all, old fellow,' he said with a grim smile. 'However, I fear the same cannot be said for Mr Davery.'

Without understanding, I made to enter the building. 'I will see if I can do anything for him.'

'I really would not take the trouble. He lies dead on that dusty floor with half his face and a good portion of his right arm missing.'

I stared at my friend in astonishment. 'He was about to fire at you. At that distance he could not have missed.'

Holmes closed the doors, took my arm and guided me away. We began to walk along the street with the snow sticking to our coats, watching for a hansom.

'It is very difficult to shoot, with a firearm that has a metal bolt hammered into the barrel,' he explained.

'That was what you did to the pistol, in our rooms? I thought you were repairing it.'

'It was a souvenir from an affair that I was concerned with, before your time. I considered it to be more useful used like this, rather than gathering rust in my trunk.'

'But I saw the drug administered to you. How did you escape its effects?'

A cab emerged from a cloud of snow. We climbed aboard and Holmes gave our destination, before he continued as if our conversation had gone uninterrupted.

'You will recall that I first learned of the compound from Professor Faye. He told me also that an antidote was known, and easily obtained. Fortunately, the necessary ingredients were already present among my chemicals, so I was able to mix and test the tincture in advance.'

We lapsed into a short silence as we watched a small crowd, appearing as ghostly figures in the wind-driven snow, enter the lighted doorway of a tavern.

'You do realise, Holmes, that some would consider you a murderer?'

He leaned back in his seat and sighed. 'We have had this conversation before, Watson, at the conclusion of the Roylott affair. My answer is unchanged. Davery's death will rob me of no sleep, I assure you. When he is discovered it will appear as suicide, which is both appropriate and ironic. It is doubtful that my presence at the Agora club will come into it since the only witness, the waiter, lived in fear of Davery for some reason and will surely not come forward. Consider also that I was nowhere near either Davery or the gun when he pulled the trigger.' He paused and sighed wearily. 'But, old friend, on such a grim day let us talk of brighter things. We can certainly look forward to the warmth of a glass of spirits in our stomachs on our return to Baker Street.'

There were occasions, during my long acquaintance with Sherlock Holmes, when a case would present itself indirectly, rather than by the usual means of a visiting client. Often, these would prove to be among the most curious, and therefore most attractive to him, to be undertaken by my friend.

At breakfast, one early April morning in that fateful year of 1891, I saw that a dark mood threatened him, probably because no new cases had recently presented themselves.

'A walk in the fresh air of St James's Park will raise your spirits,' I suggested.

'Perhaps,' he replied gloomily. 'But wait, I hear a coach near our door!' He sprang to his feet, abandoning his coffee for the view from the window. After a moment he shook his head and resumed his seat at the table.

'A married woman,' he explained, 'who seeks the jewellers' shop along the street.'

'And how,' I enquired mildly, 'did you deduce from such a brief glance that she is married?'

'She carried a newborn child.'

'And her destination?'

'She wore no wedding ring. Therefore she requires a replacement, or an adjustment to one that is ill-fitting.'

As he finished speaking the doorbell rang, repeatedly.

'A telegram,' I said. 'The impatient fellow must be in a hurry.'

'Could it not be a new client?'

It was now my turn to explain. 'The telegram boy's ring is familiar to me, and he arrived on foot or by bicycle.'

'Bravo, Watson!' Holmes clapped his hands. 'Truly, I never get your measure. I can hear Mrs Hudson scolding the lad for his impertinence.'

Soon she entered, bearing a yellow envelope. I looked on eagerly, hoping that this was something to raise his spirits further. He slit the envelope eagerly with his breakfast knife.

'It is from Mycroft.'

'You have not heard from your brother for some time.'

He dropped the form onto the table. 'He would like us to call on him, this morning.'

'We have agreed that there is nothing pressing.'
'He seems to require some assistance.'
'Is he at the Diogenes Club?'

Holmes shook his head. 'It seems that he has temporarily forsaken his Whitehall office for premises at East Cheshire Place. It is a small square, near enough to cause him no inconvenience. Come then, if you have no objection, we will go now.'

With that and pausing only for Holmes to impale the telegram on the jack knife that secured his correspondence to the mantle shelf, we took our hats and coats and went out into the sunshine.

As the hansom left us, I glanced around East Cheshire Place with curiosity. It was one of those hidden squares that are scattered all over London, and I had not known of its existence until now. It was made up of square stone buildings, and near the Trafalgar Square end of Whitehall.

Holmes preceded me up a short flight of steps and rang the bell. Presently the door was opened by an elderly servant. Holmes produced his card and the man bowed and stood aside for us. 'You are expected, gentlemen.'

He led us along a short passage. At the furthest door he stopped and knocked lightly, attracting an immediate response. Holmes and I were ushered into a dimly lit sanctum containing several chairs and a desk. Grim portraits, presumably of past Whitehall notables, adorned one wall, and green curtains covered the single window.

Mycroft Holmes greeted us both heartily. 'Sherlock, and Doctor Watson, how good of you to come so promptly.'

'It was a surprise to receive your summons,' my friend responded.

My recollections of Holmes' elder brother did not quite match the appearance of the man who stood before us. I remembered him as large and corpulent, but now he was more so. His eyes, in which I saw the greatest resemblance to my friend, were steely-grey as before.

'I am surprised to find that you have moved, Mycroft.' Holmes remarked.

'It is purely a temporary measure. My office is so full of drafts that I can no longer abide working there. This place is a little austere, but I will not be here for long.'

'Is the reason that we are here connected to your work?' Mycroft shook his head. 'No, but I have something to relate that may have some interest for you.'

Holmes looked at his brother warily. 'Pray tell us what you have in mind.'

'Would you like tea?'

We both declined.

'Very well, then.'

We took the chairs that Mycroft offered, as he sat behind the desk.

'Should we undertake this task, then who is to be our client?' Holmes enquired.

'Be patient, Sherlock. The man in the middle of this troublesome situation is Rodney Trasker, an old school chum. He has recently joined the Diogenes Club at my invitation, and I learned of his difficulties in the Strangers Room. You don't remember him at school, I suppose?'

Holmes indicated that he did not.

'No, I was forgetting. We were a little ahead of you.'

'If you would explain, Mycroft.'

'Ah yes. Trasker is one of those fortunate fellows who has never needed to find employment. His father died years ago, leaving him and his half-sister the proceeds from the sale of his rubber importing business. Consequently, Trasker spends his time managing his estate, Oaklands Hall, while his sister travels across Europe collecting botanical specimens for Kew Gardens and similar institutions.

'Some two months ago, Trasker arose in the morning to find that someone had broken into the house, although a later examination revealed that nothing had been stolen. He reported this to the local police and eventually found himself confronted by our old friend Lestrade, who came out from Scotland Yard to interview him. It transpired that a man was seen running from the house in the early hours by a local constable, who gave chase. The intruder was unfortunate enough to fall into a nearby road mender's pit and suffered a broken neck.'

'Was he known, in the area?' asked Holmes.

'Not at all. There was nothing in his pockets to identify him. He carried not so much as a handkerchief, but was later recognised as Micah Bitterfield, a known member of a spy ring in the pay of Imperial Germany. That, of course, was how Scotland Yard came to be involved, especially as it had previously been discovered that a list of our own agents working across Europe was missing from the Foreign Office.'

'I see, at last, why you have called upon me, Mycroft. What else is known about this ring?'

The elder Holmes paused, as if considering how much to disclose. 'After Bitterfield there were known to be three other members still at large. These are Heinrich Werner, Albert Derringsham and the head of the organisation, who has never been identified. Soon after the break-in, Trasker unwittingly hired Derringsham, who presented himself as a coachman. That same night he was disturbed by a noise and went down to the library to be faced with a levelled pistol held by his new coachman who was in the act of ransacking the room. Trasker managed to distract Derringsham, before striking him a fatal blow with a heavy statuette. As he lay dying, Derringsham's last words were: "I will be revenged on you, in this world or the next".'

'There,' said I, 'is where this story really begins.'

'You are correct, Doctor Watson,' Mycroft acknowledged, 'or almost so. A week or more ago, Lillette Trasker, the half-sister, arrived unannounced. This was not unusual, for she apparently does this occasionally, but rarely stays for more than a day or two. This time was different, because a delay in her journey had tired her. She was astonished to hear of her brother's recent experiences.

'Three days passed and Trasker awoke at midnight to hear her screaming. He threw on his dressing gown and ran to her room. From the window they looked down to see a coach waiting at the front of the house, and Albert Derringsham looking up at them. In an instant, the coach had gone.'

Holmes, to my surprise, laughed harshly.

'Come, Mycroft, you cannot expect me to take this seriously. It is not a difficult matter to disguise someone to look like someone else, particularly in darkness. It seems clear that Bitterfield had obtained the list, if it is connected with all this, from his associate in the Foreign Office, and for some reason was unable to pass it to Derringsham who was the next link in its journey to Berlin. Consequently, Bitterfield hid it within Oaklands Hall after informing Derringsham, who obtained employment there not long after. This is substantiated by the coachman's actions in searching the library, rather than simply robbing Mr Trasker. The only mystery here is why Mr Trasker's house was chosen for this.'

'There is more, Sherlock,' Mycroft beamed. 'There is more.'

My friend sighed. 'Pray proceed, then.'

'The following night the same thing occurred, but Trasker refused to call in the local police, saying that they would consider his complaint ridiculous and that he was capable of settling his own problems. The next night he waited in his sister's room, armed with a shotgun. The coach arrived as before, exactly at midnight, and Trasker immediately opened fire with both barrels. The coachman was blown to pieces and the horses bolted. I enquired as to any report he might have made, but he shrugged and replied that the police were unlikely to be interested in the death of a ghost.'

'Had he the presence of mind to inspect the ground?' Holmes asked.

Mycroft shook his head. 'I doubt if that occurred to him, Sherlock. The man was unnerved.'

'Most regrettable,' said Holmes thoughtfully.

'There is yet more. Trasker, having felt unwell for some time, spent much of the following day resting. With the coming of evening he ate a light meal and retired early, but was again awakened by his sister. Half-wakeful, for he had taken a sleeping draught, he saw that the coach had returned. He was horrified to see the coachman, completely unscathed, looking up at him! Then the coach swiftly departed.'

'When was this?' I asked.

'The night before last. Yesterday morning Trasker came up to London and I met him in the Diogenes Club, as I told you. Early today he telegraphed his sister to enquire whether the coachman had appeared last night. She replied that he had, but passed on after staring up at the window. Trasker informed me soon after.'

Holmes' attention appeared to have wavered to one of the portraits behind his brother, but I knew that his keen mind missed nothing.

'So, Mycroft,' he said at last, 'you would like me to visit your friend Trasker, at Oaklands Hall, to retrieve this list?

Mycroft nodded his assent. 'Find out as much as you can, about as much as you can, dear boy. I have no doubt that there is much hidden in all this. Had I the energy, and the time, I would be meticulous in my investigation.'

'I have no doubt of it,' Holmes said with a touch of irony.

'There is a train to Richmond at twelve fifteen. If you hurry, you should catch it.'

'Is Mr Trasker expecting me?'

'You and Doctor Watson, yes. He returned to Surrey this morning, after I replied to his wire to tell him that you would be arriving later. You see, Sherlock, the enormous confidence that I have in you?'

#

We found a hansom quickly. My friend said little during the journey back to Baker Street. His deep contemplation was evident.

'Be so good as to hand me my Bradshaw from the shelf,' he said as we settled into our chairs. After turning a few pages he asked, to my surprise,

'Are you hungry, Watson?'

'Moderately. Lunch time approaches, but we will miss our train if we fail to leave within the next ten minutes.'

He stood and replaced the book. 'I have no intention of catching it. A later train will serve just as well. Meanwhile, I am curious about Mycroft's attitude. Therefore, after Mrs Hudson's veal and ham pie, I would be grateful if you would return to East Cheshire Place.'

'What on Earth for?' I retorted.

'I simply want you to watch my brother's office for an hour, before returning to report to me. I noticed a narrow passage at the other side of the square, which will provide adequate concealment if you are careful. On no account be noticed.' He turned towards the door. 'But here is our good lady with lunch. Let us eat well, before we look into this affair.'

Shortly after, a hansom took me back to East Cheshire Place, completely mystified as to why Holmes had sent me on this errand. I found the passage easily enough and settled into a position from where I could see the offices across the square. I was resigned to an uneventful hour of confronting a rather depressing façade, when it struck me that it had altered. The green curtains had gone from the window of Mycroft's office! Presently the door opened, and a succession of burly men carrying the desk, chairs and the portraits appeared. I watched as they marched in line, disappearing in the direction of Trafalgar Square, where Holmes and I had entered, earlier. All was still for several minutes before a rotund bowler-hatted man, possibly a foreman, left the premises after locking the door.

I continued my observations for a further ten minutes, at a loss to explain this development. Had Holmes known, or suspected, that this would happen, or was it something else that he intended me to see here? Had Mycroft been recalled to Whitehall because of some sudden crisis? These and other possibilities filled my mind as I left East Cheshire Place. I wondered what Holmes would make of it.

Mid-afternoon found me once more seated comfortably in our rooms. I had described to my friend the curious activity that I had witnessed in East Cheshire Place and he now considered, thoughtfully smoking his clay pipe.

'You did well, Watson,' he said finally. 'I see now why Mycroft conducted this charade.'

'I confess that I am puzzled by his actions.'

'Do you recall that the foreign spy, Micah Bitterfield, broke into Trasker's house for no apparent reason?'

'Of course. You believed that he had hidden a secret document there.'

'Indeed. How did he come by that document?'

'Your brother indicated that it had been stolen from the Foreign Office.'

'Precisely. Therefore, there is a German agent, or someone sympathetic to Germany, working in the Foreign Office. Naturally then, Mycroft would arrange to retrieve the document away from there, because his plans might be overheard or discovered. It is very like him to take such precautions, and we can now proceed with the certainty that the German agent is unaware of our connection with this affair.'

I had no time to reply before Holmes put out his pipe and indicated his travelling bag, placed near the door.

'It would be as well to get a few things together, doctor. Our train leaves Paddington in less than an hour.'

The journey was a short one. I can remember Holmes making but one remark while we travelled, as the open fields and leafy glades replaced the smoky city buildings.

'At all costs, Watson, we must keep the existence of the hidden list from everyone at Oaklands Hall.'

'Would not Lestrade have mentioned it to Trasker, during his interview?'

'Not at all. The subject of that exchange was the breaking and entering of the house, nothing more.'

We pulled into Richmond station soon after and walked out into a tree-lined lane to where a trap awaited us in the charge of a huge, hulking man with an unkempt beard. To my surprise he smiled warmly and shook Holmes by the hand.

'Mr Holmes, it is good to see you again,' he said, 'and your companion is Doctor Watson, I am sure.'

We also shook hands and Holmes explained. 'This, Watson, is Detective-Sergeant Querry, who works closely with Lestrade. I met him a short while ago at the Yard.'

'Inspector Lestrade is aware of the strange happenings at Oaklands Hall,' Querry said. 'When Mr Trasker's groom fell ill, the inspector managed to get me in as a temporary replacement.'

'I must congratulate Lestrade on his astuteness,' Holmes commented as we climbed aboard the trap. 'I would be greatly in your debt, Querry, if you would tell me as much as you can about the house and its occupants.'

Querry took up the reins and the horse at once broke into a trot. 'Oaklands Hall is a Stuart mansion,' he began, 'owned by the Trasker family for several generations. It is surrounded by forest and a wide expanse of open field and is maintained by the income from foreign investments.'

'Most interesting, but what of the present occupants?'

'Well, there is Mr Trasker and his sister, or rather, half-sister, and two guests who arrived by the earlier train. They are Mr Cromer and Mr Fullerton, but as yet I know nothing else of them. The staff, apart from myself, comprises of Gerrard, the butler, the cook and two maids.'

'Thank you,' said Holmes. 'Since arriving there, have you seen anything or anyone out of the ordinary?'

Querry urged the horse into a gallop. 'There is the business of the coach of course. Mr Trasker is looking rather unwell of late, so I am wondering if he is more upset by this than he appears. As for strangers, Mr Holmes, I have seen none save the gentleman who asked directions from Miss Lillette, earlier today.'

'Where was this?'

'There is a gate at the side of the house. Miss Lillette was picking flowers for the table, as she sometimes does, when the gentleman walked past.'

'He appeared on foot?'

'He did. I imagine him to have been a hiker, for quite a few pass the house on their way to Little Chillington, the village two miles further along the road.'

'Is that a large place?' I interrupted.

'None of the villages are, around here, doctor. There is only the church, an inn, the livery stables, the Post Office, various small shops and a few farm labourers' cottages.'

The road was quiet, except for the occasional farm cart. We passed a wide field, which Querry referred to as The Old Deer Park, and water that he called Syon Reach, where herons watchfully awaited their prey.

'Does this road pass the house and continue through the village?' Holmes asked.

'It does, sir. The house is around the next bend. We will be there soon.'

Oaklands Hall stood a short way back from the road, so that it was possible to pass through the narrow courtyard before joining the road again at a point further on. A wide strip of lawn separated the house from the road.

Querry brought the horse to a gentle halt. Holmes was quickly on his hands and knees, examining the area around the front door.

'Most interesting,' was his only comment as he stood up.

The iron-studded door was opened almost immediately by the butler, as Querry took the trap around the back of the house to the stables.

'Mr Sherlock Holmes and Doctor Watson,' the butler intoned at once. 'Please come in, gentlemen.'

We had given up our hats and coats, when a short, balding man rushed up to us. His eyes appeared sunk in his head and I detected a tremor in both his handshake and his voice.

'Trasker, my good sirs, Rodney Trasker,' he explained breathlessly. 'It is so good of you to visit us, and a pleasure to meet you both.'

'My brother speaks well of you,' Holmes replied. 'I am here to help in any way that I can.'

Mr Trasker glanced over his shoulder hurriedly, to ensure that none of the other people entering the hall could hear.

'I beg of you, do not tell the others of the coachman in the night. Apart from the staff, my sister alone knows what I have witnessed, and I have no wish to be thought mad by my friends.'

'You may rely upon us, but I must insist upon a private conversation after dinner. Perhaps there is a room where we will not be disturbed?'

'My study should serve for that.'

'Gentlemen,' interrupted a lady in a startling red costume. 'Welcome to Oaklands Hall.'

'My sister, Lillette,' Trasker introduced. 'Mr Sherlock Holmes and Doctor Watson.'

She was an extremely handsome woman with high cheekbones and hair as black as a raven's wing. Her face shone with the vibrant energy of a strong personality.

'And here,' she continued, drawing in two onlookers, 'are our other guests. May I introduce Mr Forsyth Cromer,' a thin-faced man gave us a rather disapproving look, 'and Mr Gabriel Fullerton.'

A shorter, swarthy man stepped forward to shake our hands.

'Hunt, do you?' Mr Cromer asked me.

'I have little time to spare sir,' said I, 'for my London practice is invariably busy.'

'Pity,' he replied. 'I hear there are fallow deer in the woods around here.'

He turned away abruptly and Holmes, who had been talking to the others, followed him with his eyes.

'I think, Watson, that if someone will be good enough to show us to our rooms, we will refresh ourselves and change for dinner.'

The butler, Gerrard, showed us to comfortable, if rather small, rooms. I quickly unpacked and changed, before meeting Holmes on the landing.

We ate at a long table in a hall hung with mediaeval shields and weapons. To my most pleasant surprise Miss Lillette, wearing a purple dress, was seated next to me, and maintained lively conversation throughout the meal. I heard snatches of the talk between the others and learned that Mr Cromer was a London solicitor and Mr Fullerton an insurance broker. Much that was spoken was of hunting and fishing, except for the exchange between Holmes and Mr Trasker, concerning the ever-changing scene in London.

At the conclusion of the meal, Mr Trasker approached his sister and spoke quietly. She nodded vigorously and led the other two from the room.

'They have gone to the games room,' he told us. 'I explained that we are likely to be late in joining them. She will see that they are kept amused at cards.'

'Excellent,' said Holmes. 'Let us repair to your study.'

We crossed a stone-flagged corridor to a room that proved to be much as I expected. Dark panelling and bookshelves surrounded a desk and several armchairs near an unlit fire. Only after we had settled ourselves and lit cigars did Holmes begin his questioning.

'Mycroft has explained much of your situation to me, Mr Trasker,' said he, 'but there are still a few points about which I am not quite clear. Pray take your time in answering and try to do so as accurately as you can.' He leaned forward suddenly for Mr Trasker had swayed in his chair, almost dropping his cigar. 'My dear fellow, you are not well! Watson, a brandy, quickly!'

I poured from the decanter on a side-table and administered a half-glass to our host, but it was quite a quarter of an hour before he was restored sufficiently to continue.

'I feel stronger now, gentlemen,' he said in a quivering voice. 'I am grateful for your assistance.'

'For how long have you experienced these seizures?' I asked him.

'I cannot recall exactly, for my memory seems affected. I sought no help, for I have always had a morbid fear of hospitals. However, doctor, I would be grateful for your diagnosis.'

His eyes held a vacant expression that concerned me greatly, as did his appearance. But I had met these symptoms before.

'I must ask you, Mr Trasker, without intending any offence - do you take opium?'

'Never,' he stated definitely. 'I have seen others ruined by it. That was warning enough.'

'Quite. Let me consider the matter. I may have to consult my books in Baker Street but be assured that I can help.'

'I am already indebted to you,' he said gratefully. 'But now, Mr Holmes, I feel able to continue.'

I refilled his glass and poured for Holmes and myself, before my friend began.

'First the coach. Are you satisfied that it is the same coach, at every appearance?'

Mr Trasker nodded. 'I am sure of it. As you will know, I emptied both barrels of my shotgun at its driver. The following night the coachman seemed unharmed, but the damage to the coach was evident.'

'And was it familiar to you?'

'It was a landau that I had never seen before.'

'The horses?'

'Two large black beasts. There are many like them in use around this district. I could not tell if they were local.'

'Thank you.' Holmes considered for a moment. 'This road that passes the house, it runs from Richmond through Little Chillington, does it not?'

'Indeed, and through several other villages further on.'

'If one were to pass this house in the direction of the village, is there a way to return without passing the house again?'

'There are many tracks winding through the forest. It is possible to return to the road nearer to Richmond.'

'So I had supposed. I understand that it was from your sister's room that you saw the coachman on all occasions.'

'That is so. It is the only room that looks down on that part of the courtyard.'

Holmes put down his empty glass. 'It is imperative that Doctor Watson and I are installed there, ready to anticipate the coachman. You will not be disturbed tonight, Mr Trasker.'

Our host was noticeably relieved. 'I will make the arrangements. Lillette will sleep elsewhere. No one will go near that room until morning.'

'Capital!'

Mr Trasker left us, and we finished our cigars. He reappeared, much improved, a short while later.

'It is done,' he said.

Presently we joined the others, to find that Miss Lillette had already retired as she intended to take one of the mares out early. Mr Cromer and Mr Fullerton drained their glasses, agreeing that the journey from London had been tiring. I suggested to Mr Trasker that he also should take to his bed soon to conserve his strength, and he readily agreed. So it was that at half past eleven Holmes and I found ourselves in the room previously occupied by Miss Lillette, watching from the window awaiting an unknown foe with our hands never far from our revolvers.

The road was quiet, except for leaves rustling in the faint breeze. Midnight came swiftly, with Holmes' expectations mounting, but the hour passed without incident.

'We will wait a short while longer,' he whispered.

I found it hard to stay awake, but Holmes seemed as alert as always. I heard a horse approaching and a new tenseness rose, but it was a lone rider upon a weary mount, and I presumed him to be a local man returning from Richmond.

Soon after, a family of deer strayed across the road before returning to the forest.

'The coachman will not appear now,' Holmes said quietly.

'An unexpected disappointment.'

'To the contrary, this night has turned out exactly as I expected.'

'You foresaw this?'

'I was certain of it.'

'You know what is happening here?' I asked in astonishment.

'Much begins to make sense. Now I suggest that we return to our rooms to salvage what we can of our night's sleep.'

We made our way through the dark and silent house, carrying a single candle. As we parted I saw in that poor light the glitter in my friend's eyes that meant, unmistakeably, that he had caught the scent.

I went down to breakfast early the next morning to find Holmes already halfway through his eggs and bacon. I joined him, ordering the same together with a pot of strong coffee. Of Mr Cromer and Mr Fullerton there was no sign, and we agreed that they had probably not yet risen. Gerrard informed us that it was Mr Trasker's custom to take a walk before breakfast, but we would see him later.

Miss Lillette strode into the room wearing riding clothes, and we exchanged greetings.

'Doctor Watson and I saw nothing last night,' Holmes told her. 'Perhaps this business will die out of its own accord.'

'I do hope so,' she said with concern, 'for Rodney's sake above all. He really is not well but refuses to consult a doctor.'

'Doctor Watson may be able to prescribe something that will help.'

She removed her riding cap and shook out her hair. 'Again, we are grateful to you both.'

'I wonder if we could borrow the trap for the morning. There is nothing to be done here, and the prospect of a walk around your charming village might be agreeable. Will Mr Trasker be long returning, do you think?'

'He may be, since his walks vary according to his mood. But there is no need to wait, Mr Holmes. You have only to tell Querry, the groom, that I would be obliged if he would prepare it for you.'

Holmes thanked her and she left us. When our meal was finished, we went directly to the stables, where Querry was rubbing down the horse that Miss Lillette had recently exercised. Holmes said that there was little to report, and he replied likewise, adding that he was keeping a close watch on

Mr Cromer and Mr Fullerton. The trap was soon ready, and we left in the direction of Little Chillington.

We progressed at a moderate pace, and Holmes peered around in every direction.

'What is it that you are looking for, Holmes?'

'I will know it when I see it.'

We passed a long curve before he spoke again.

'Rein in, Watson!'

'Near that old barn?'

'Exactly there.'

As we came to a halt he sprang to the ground, walking up and down in front of the structure before returning with a frown upon his face.

'You found nothing?' I enquired.

'No. Its dilapidated appearance suggested that the barn is no longer used, but it has merely been neglected.'

I knew that my friend would explain when he was ready, so I said nothing more. Shortly after, we sat at a rough wooden table outside the village inn.

'Two pints of your best ale if you please, landlord!' Holmes called cheerfully to the man who approached.

Red-faced and bald, he signalled his acknowledgement. 'Right away, sir.'

Soon, he delivered two foaming tankards.

'Do you know this area well?' Holmes asked him.

'Lived here all my life, sir.'

'We are from a London establishment specialising in the restoration of disused property in provincial districts. A request was received for us to survey an abandoned building in this area, but we have accidentally left the details behind. Do you, by any chance, know of such a building? We have driven around for miles but have found nothing.'

The landlord scratched his head. 'No sir, I cannot think where that could be. The only abandoned building I know of is the old church on Middlemire Road. It was struck by lightning some ten years ago and never repaired because folk hereabouts attend St Thaddeus, here in the village.'

Holmes nodded. 'Well, as we have come all this way, we may as well look at it. How is it reached, from here?'

'You go straight through the village,' the man pointed, 'then watch for the signpost to the left.'

We found Middlemire Road easily. I slowed the horse and we turned onto a wide track. It was largely overgrown, probably since the damage to the church, but still my friend saw at once that something had passed by recently.

'There are disturbed and broken bushes,' he observed. 'It may be that this is the place we seek.'

'But what are we looking for, Holmes?'

'We have found it, I think.'

The undergrowth fell away, revealing an untended field. Many gravestones leaned precariously, and a weathered stone angel gazed down at us. The church, or as much as remained of it, stood near the track.

'Half the roof has gone,' I observed. 'Why are we here?'

'We are seeking answers.'

I tethered the horse and we made our way along a short path. Holmes pulled open the tall entrance door and the rusted hinges protested loudly. We walked cautiously into a vast chamber, disturbing birds that roosted among the rafters.

Holmes examined the dusty floor. 'We are in the right place, Watson. Here are the tracks of a man and two horses. Also, there are wheel marks that lead further into the church and back, several times.'

'The coach?'

'I shall be surprised to find otherwise. It had to be stored out of sight, between visits to Oaklands Hall.'

Our footfalls echoed back at us. The air was heavy with the smell of decay. Sunlight streamed through the pierced roof, revealing scattered slates upon the altar. The marks in the dust led to a large alcove near the sanctuary.

'You were right, Holmes!' I cried. A black landau stood, deep in shadow.

'There we see the damage from Mr Trasker's shotgun. The soft top and wooden coachwork have been badly torn in places.' He walked slowly around the coach. 'But look, here are traces of wax, such as I discovered outside Oaklands Hall on our arrival. It now becomes clear how the coachman survived the blast.'

'Some sort of shield? I hardly think it would be strong enough to withstand two barrels.'

Holmes peered into the darkness. 'Aha!' he cried after a moment.

The broken effigy of a man lay sprawled upon the flagstones. A few feet away stood several others, sinister in the half-light, undamaged and moulded in the same likeness.

'These are undoubtedly fashioned to appear to be Derringsham, who Mr Trasker killed during the burglary,' my friend said. 'The damaged remains are of course from the shotgun blast, later.'

'Holmes, this cannot be. Mycroft mentioned that Mr Trasker stated that the coachman looked up at him. A wax model cannot move of its own accord.'

'I think I can show how it could do so with some assistance.'

'Holes have been cut in the front of the soft top, near where it joins the coachwork,' I observed.

'Indeed, that is so that the horses could be guided from inside, by a man lying full length. This could not be sustained, so probably the effigy was set up immediately before approaching Oaklands Hall, and then normal driving resumed as soon as the house was out of sight. But look,' he bent over the damaged figure, 'at the neck and arms of this fellow.'

'They have wires running through them, like puppets!'

'So, the shotgun blast destroyed but one of several wax effigies, and its movements had been guided like those of a marionette. The darkness of course, aided the deception.'

'Trasker has been treated cruelly.'

'I suspect, Watson, that there is more cruelty in this.' Holmes looked into the landau. 'Halloa! It appears that I have missed something.'

'What more have you found?'

'Blood,' he answered.

I peered beneath the covering. Dark stains marked the floor.

'So,' I concluded, 'the driver did not escape Mr Trasker's shotgun, after all.'

'Not entirely. He will have some injuries. I confess a certain admiration of this man's courage.'

'My dear fellow! What can you mean?'

'He returned to Oaklands Hall after the shooting, not knowing whether he would again face that danger. We must therefore conclude that we are dealing with a brave, although ruthless, man. You will understand this, having been under fire yourself.'

A recollection of the Battle of Maiwand came to me. 'Indeed, but these are our country's enemies.'

'They are, and that is why we shall bring them to ruin. There are two more calls to make, doctor, and then we return to Oaklands Hall.'

Soon we were in Little Chillington once more.

'If you would care to wait for me, I will not be long.' Holmes sprang from the trap and made off down the street. I tethered the horse and had begun to inspect the rose gardens in front of some charming ivy-covered cottages when he called my name.

We left the village for Oaklands Hall with the horse eager to get into its stride.

'Did you learn anything of significance?' I asked.

'For the consideration of a half-sovereign, the boy at the livery stable was most forthcoming. Although he could not remember the times with certainty, he confirmed that a foreign gentlemen, has on several occasions left his grey mount to be cared for late at night, while he hired two black mares for short periods.'

'He exchanged his own horse for two to pull the coach!'

'Exactly. My other call was to the Post Office, to send a wire.'

I recognised about him that air that meant the case was nearing its end, and so asked nothing more. At lunch he spoke little, answering the remarks of Mr Cromer and Mr Fullerton with few words. We repaired to a sitting room shortly after, where we found the early editions. Presently, we heard Mr Trasker and Miss Lillette in conversation in the entrance hall, and I assumed that they had lunched elsewhere. Then Gerrard brought a telegram for Holmes which I assumed to be from Lestrade, though my friend confirmed only that it was an answer to an earlier enquiry.

'I fear that we must cut short our stay,' he said with some urgency as he laid down the newspaper and put the folded form in his pocket. 'Come, Watson, we must pack our things before asking Mr Trasker to allow Querry to drive us to Richmond Station.'

This we did, at once. If my surprise was evident however, then Mr Trasker's was more so.

'But Mr Holmes,' he exclaimed, 'the threat persists. Nothing has been solved.'

'Regarding this, I think you will find that the future holds very little trouble for you,' Holmes said in a reassuring tone. 'If you watch again from Miss Lillette's room tonight, you will see that there is now nothing to fear.'

Miss Lillette was equally surprised but accepted the situation well. She remarked that our efforts were appreciated and stood next to her brother, watching Querry drive us away at a fast trot.

Once out of sight of the house, Holmes informed Querry of all that we had discovered.

'The wire that I received was not from Lestrade, as I saw that Watson had supposed, but from a London company called McMichaels,' he explained. 'I saw their mark stamped upon the broken effigy in the church. They were kind enough to furnish me with a description of the recent customer who ordered the wax models.'

'Then the case is solved,' replied Querry.

'There is a little more, yet. I would be grateful if you would wait at Richmond Station while we deposit our bags and I wire Lestrade, before taking us back as far as the cluster of oaks that stand a short way before the house. Tonight should see the end of all this.'

No doubt Querry was surprised, but if so, he did not show it. As we reached the outskirts of the town, he regarded Holmes with silent admiration.

I deposited our luggage while Holmes went to the telegraph office. Very soon we were on our way back to the house. I remember well his words to Querry: 'It would be as well to keep watch from midnight onwards and enter when you see that Inspector Lestrade has arrived.'

Querry acknowledged this with a faintly puzzled air. We reached the oaks and watched the trap out of sight before entering the shelter of the trees.

'We have some hours to wait, Watson,' Holmes said when he had ascertained that we could not be seen from the road. 'While in Richmond I anticipated our need for sustenance.'

At that he produced ham sandwiches with mustard and two small bottles of ale. We ate and drank later, at twilight, before making our way to a hiding place among the tall grass opposite Oaklands Hall.

We crouched, whispering occasionally, for what seemed an age. From time to time we heard animals in the bushes, and the calls of nesting birds above us.

Full darkness had fallen some time earlier. Now Holmes took out his pocket watch and tilted it to catch the light of the moon. 'It is almost time. He will come from the Richmond direction.'

Moments later the quiet of the countryside was disturbed. A landau drawn by two black horses appeared and drew to a halt, a short distance from the house. I saw that my friend had interpreted the situation correctly, for the driver alighted and replaced himself with the stiff figure of a wax model, arranging it so that the limbs and head moved at his bidding. He placed his hat upon the head of the effigy and draped a cape around it, before disappearing inside the coach.

'He must have some experience,' Holmes said quietly, 'as a puppeteer or some such thing.'

'It cannot be easy to drive horses from that position.'

'Indeed not. We must proceed carefully. As the coach comes to a halt beneath the window, run over and hold the horses' heads. I will account for the man inside.'

As we left our concealment with our weapons drawn, I glimpsed Mr Trasker's silhouette, framed in the window above. The horses were easily calmed. I held them with my free hand as the coach door was wrenched open.

'Good morning, Mr Heinrich Werner!' cried Holmes. 'Be so good as to come out and present yourself.'

'I will take care of him, Mr Holmes,' said Lestrade from the darkness.

A man of middle height stood up, to be swiftly handcuffed by the inspector. The four constables accompanying him advanced towards the house.

In response to Lestrade's violent knocking, Gerrard appeared at the door in his nightshirt. The inspector spoke briefly and we were instantly admitted.

Werner was bundled into the sitting room, where we were quickly joined by Mr Trasker. I was appalled by the sight of him. His eyes seemed to have sunk further into his head and he trembled noticeably. His unshaven face was grey, and his movements unsteady.

'Mr Holmes,' he stammered, 'and Inspector Lestrade! And you have a prisoner! Is this the end at last?'

'Not quite,' Holmes replied. 'But nearly so. You have but a few moments to wait.'

Mr Cromer and Mr Fullerton, in night attire, entered the room, both bleary-eyed and angry looking from their disturbed sleep. Miss Lillette appeared after them in a blue dressing gown, her expression one of mild surprise because of our reappearance.

'Gentlemen,' she said in a voice without weariness, 'what is the meaning of this? Who is this man?'

'His name is Heinrich Werner,' Holmes answered. 'He is part of the foreign spy ring responsible for your brother's illness and other troubles. The effect was greatly enhanced by the regular doses of the strong opiate that has been administered, probably in his food.' He paused, undoubtedly for effect since my friend could never resist a touch of melodrama. 'But then, you are already aware of these things, are you not, Miss Lillette?'

Trasker looked as if he had been struck by a thunderbolt. 'Lillette!' he cried, 'Is this true? Dear God, no!'

Her mask slipped immediately, for there was now no escaping the truth. 'I saw the power that is in Germany and will sweep through this island and subdue it,' she spat viciously. 'I have spent much time in that country and have become as one of its people. Did you know, Rodney, did father tell you that my mother, his second wife, was German? Oh, you would never have believed it, for she posed successfully as an Englander, but her heart was always in her homeland. She would have given this country up for her own in an instant, and so would I.'

'But, to make your own flesh and blood suffer ....' I said in astonishment.

Her face and voice were now unlike those of the woman who had welcomed us to this house. Gone was the pleasant smile, the gaiety and the warmth, replaced by a stone-faced glare and eyes of obsidian.

'Only our father connects us,' she said harshly. 'It is nothing.'

Querry, who had entered quietly, gripped her arm from behind. A small pearl-handled pistol fell half-drawn from her dressing-gown to the floor near Lestrade's feet. She screamed her anger at us in German.

The inspector picked up the weapon and gestured to the constables. Both prisoners were taken from the room.

'I acted as soon as I received your wire, Mr Holmes,' he explained. 'The constables are local men who have brought a police wagon. Those two will be in the cells within the hour. We hid in the woods until the coach made its appearance, as you suggested.'

'I was aware of it,' my friend replied. 'Dr Watson and I were concealed quite close to you. I saw you once, and your companions twice, but I must congratulate you, nevertheless. I could not predict how matters would end, once Miss Lillette had been exposed.'

'She is the head of the ring, then?'

Holmes nodded. 'Her arrival was delayed, which is how Derringsham's attempt came about. Since then, she has manipulated everything. The gradual poisoning of her brother made him susceptible to the apparent supernatural appearance of the coachman.'

'But to what purpose?' I asked.

'She wished to have her brother committed to an asylum. Once he was out of the way, she could search for the hidden list undisturbed. To simply kill him would have brought the unwelcome attention of a police investigation.'

'But it is still missing,' remarked Lestrade.

'A problem for others to solve,' Holmes smiled. 'Our part in this is finished.'

#

The afternoon of the following day found us in the Strangers Room of the Diogenes Club.

'You first suspected her, of course, when Querry mentioned the man he saw her speaking to at the gate.' Mycroft said when he had considered Holmes' account.

Holmes nodded. 'That night the coachman failed to appear, after the arrival of Watson and myself. He could only have known of our presence if he had been warned by someone inside the house. Querry was adamant that there had been no other strangers in the area, and recognised Werner as the man seen talking to Miss Lillette.'

'Trasker has taken this rather badly. His nerves were always unsteady, but repeated doses of that drug together with the constant reappearance of a man who he thought he had killed came close to unhinging him completely. I have arranged for his servants to take temporary positions elsewhere, and for his horses to be cared for at a neighbouring farm, while he embarks upon a long sea voyage to recuperate.'

'Let us hope that he does so completely,' said I.

'The list, I take it, was not found?' Holmes enquired.

Mycroft looked out on Pall Mall for a long moment, and to my surprise turned back to us smiling. 'I had Oaklands Hall searched thoroughly. Nothing was discovered, so it is unlikely that it ever will be. I do not think it something that we should trouble ourselves about however, particularly as the traitor in the Foreign Office has now been discovered and dealt with.'

It struck me as strange, that Holmes' brother should dismiss so important a matter lightly. His expression, and his secretive air, stayed in my memory as we returned to Baker Street.

They came to mind again after breakfast next morning, as my friend passed me one of the early editions that he had been reading.

'What do you make of this, Watson?' he asked, as he had many times before.

I read that Oaklands Hall had burned to the ground in the early hours, only ashes remained.

I looked up and met Holmes' expressionless gaze.

Neither of us spoke, but we knew each other's thoughts.

It has to be remembered that some of the cases undertaken by my friend Sherlock Holmes have never reached the general public. This is usually because of his reluctance to reveal some element therein, to avoid embarrassment to someone concerned in the events that transpired or for less obvious reasons of his own. The following account is one that I was at first forbidden to relate, but on repeating my request recently it was met with an indifferent shrug. I therefore now set it before the reader, with Holmes' approval.

#

One cool spring morning I stood looking down onto the bustle of Baker Street, lighting my first pipe of the day after what had been a rather silent breakfast.

'What do you see that is so amusing, Watson?' asked Holmes suddenly. I heard him replace his coffee cup, and in a moment, he stood beside me.

'How did you know I was amused?'

'My dear fellow, when I see your smiling face reflected in the window, it is not a difficult conclusion to arrive at.'

I pointed, with my smouldering pipe. 'I was observing those three Greek priests, shuffling along across the street. I was reminded of the Three Wise Men.'

'Three Wise Men?'
'Those in the Christmas story.'

'Not so, old fellow, that is a common misconception. The Bible does not, in fact, mention the number of Wise Men, kings or whatever the visitors were. Their number is purely a tradition of the church. Furthermore, the descriptive word in the original Greek translation was the equivalent of astrologers, rather than Wise Men, and these are strongly disapproved of elsewhere in the Scriptures, since they practised the forbidden foretelling of the future.'

'Good heavens!' I exclaimed. 'Are you sure of this, Holmes?'

'You have only to stretch out your hand and pick up the Bible, which stands next to my Bradshaw on the bookshelf, to confirm it.'

I was about to do this, feeling slightly ashamed for doubting my friend's accuracy, yet outraged at his apparent disregard for tradition, when we were both distracted by the clang of the doorbell. We glanced at each other and stood in silence, as Mrs Hudson admitted our visitor and brought him up the stairs. A moment later the door opened and she announced:

'Mr Fortesque Collins, gentlemen,' before withdrawing.

The man who entered was of a truly formidable appearance. A huge, hulking figure, his expression was one of sadness, yet there was also an air of suppressed anger about him. He wore a waistcoat ill-matched to his other attire, and I noticed that, although he had no beard, his moustache had been allowed to become straggling and unkempt.

'Come in, sir,' Holmes said by way of welcome, 'I am Sherlock Holmes, and this is my friend and associate, Doctor John Watson.'

Mr Collins hung up his hat and joined us around the fire. He shook both our hands and lowered himself into an armchair at Holmes' indication. I thought that he looked neglected and distinctly uncomfortable, as he rubbed his hands together against the chill that had persisted into early May.

This did not escape Holmes' notice. 'Perhaps some tea, or coffee if you prefer?'

'No, no, thank you, sir,' our visitor replied rather breathlessly. 'I have come to consult you on a rather unusual matter.'

'Pray enlighten us,' Holmes smiled. 'We are accustomed here to much that is out of the ordinary.'

Mr Collins produced a crumpled sheet of paper, which he unfolded and passed to my friend. Holmes held it towards me so that, by leaning sideways, I could read it also:

Mr Fortesque Collins. Your loss has been felt, even as far away as the Hereafter. If you will attend the Langham Hotel, at 7:30pm on May the third, it may be that your grief will be eased somewhat.

'There is no signature,' Holmes observed. 'Do you already know the identity of the sender?'

'I do not!' Mr Collins said emphatically. 'I received this in the early post this morning. It is a clear reference to my late wife, who I lost a year ago. I have already enquired at the hotel, to ascertain the meaning of this outrage.'

'And what did you discover?'

'I was told that a meetings room had indeed been reserved, for tomorrow evening.'

'For what purpose, to be so outrageous?' I began, but Holmes held up a hand to silence me.

'To conduct a séance! I tell you, sirs, I do not believe in such things, and consider them an insult to the dead. I do not want my poor late wife's memory tarnished by some sideshow performance.'

'You have my sympathy,' said Holmes. 'I, too, do not believe in supernatural experiences, though several past cases have been represented to me as such. Nevertheless, you have decided to attend this gathering, for why would you be here otherwise? In what way can we assist you?'

'I would like you gentlemen to accompany me to expose this, for a crime is what it is. The object of these performances is always to extract money from a gullible audience - they cause heartbreak compounded by fraud. I know your reputation, Mr Holmes, and I believe you to be the man to save and enlighten the victims, if we may call them such.'

Holmes said nothing, and we both waited.

'Mr Collins,' he asked presently, 'are you a rich man?'

'I am a grocer. My business yields enough profit to feed and clothe me, but little more.'

'Then does it not strike you as strange, that someone who knows something of your affairs - your address, the passing of your wife - should set up a scheme to defraud you? The sender of this letter must surely be aware that you are in no position to pay out a large sum.'

Our visitor looked puzzled, and then shrugged. 'I suppose you are right. That is curious, but on the other hand we do not know who we are dealing with. It could be my barber, or the man living above the shop next to mine, in Stepney.'

'Indeed. There is clearly some mystery here. Very well, Doctor Watson' - he glanced in my direction and I nodded my assent - 'and myself will meet you at the Langham Hotel, and between the three of us we will see if we can reveal this little circus for what it truly is.'

#

'You have surprised me, Holmes,' I remarked after Mr Collins had left. 'I expected you to dismiss this case.'

He gave a short laugh. 'Ha! You must have noticed the shortage of problems to come my way recently. I feel a restlessness coming on that I would at one time have dispelled with the cocaine bottle, but you have barred me from that escape. In any event, Mr Collins' situation appears to have some unusual aspects. This would not be the first case to surprise us with its development.'

The following evening found us alighting from a hansom in Langham Place. Waning sunlight glinted on the many windows of the hotel as we crossed the street to where Mr Collins stood waiting. Despite his disbelief in the forthcoming proceedings he showed some nervousness, pacing the short distance from the hotel entrance to the nearest lamp standard and back repeatedly. He came to an abrupt halt as he saw us, and I noticed that he was dressed exactly as before. This indicated to me, as it would have to Holmes had we not known already, that our client no longer had a good woman looking after him.

'Good evening, gentlemen,' Mr Collins said rather grimly. 'I have observed that a mixed party has already gone before us. Unless I am mistaken, the room to the left of the entrance hall is our destination.'

'You have already enquired?' Holmes asked.

'Not at all, but the more expensively-dressed guests are those that proceed straight ahead, into the foyer.'

'Your use of your powers of observation is admirable,' Holmes remarked with a trace of surprise.

We quickly discovered that Mr Collins was correct. In a semi-darkened room we found ourselves seated with six others around a circular table. We could see little of our surroundings, but I gained the impression that they lacked some of the luxury that I had glimpsed as we entered. This was a room reserved for such meetings as this, or perhaps of merchants or tradesmen. There was a coolness about the air here, and a deadly hush had settled upon everyone except Holmes, who I felt was already struggling to restrain his mirth.

A very small man, surely a midget, appeared from behind the thick curtain before us, and walked around the room to the door, which he locked with the explanation: 'We must not be disturbed.'

I sensed that Holmes had seen some significance in this, but before I could ask the room darkened further with the unseen extinguishing of the remaining gas mantles. A murmur passed through the assembly.

From behind the curtain, the same voice announced: 'You are now in the presence of Madam Myra, who is your bridge to the world to come.'

I distinctly felt Holmes, sitting in the chair beside me, quiver. That he was enjoying this charade, I had no doubt.

A woman, bearing a single candle that was held to light up her face, seemed to glide across the curtain. She stopped near its centre and turned to us, placing the candle on a pedestal that I had failed to notice.

'Welcome,' she intoned in a husky voice, 'to all you who grieve for the departed. Tonight, I will attempt to re-unite you with your loved ones, if only briefly. But there are always other occasions - the spirits are always near if we truly search for them.'

The curtain behind her parted slightly, to reveal a candelabrum of gas jets that immediately burst into life. She was not a young woman, but her face was well rouged, and her eyebrows trimmed to give her an almost Oriental appearance. Her lustrous black hair, probably false I thought, hung to the shoulders of her theatrical costume. In the shadow of the background light, she did indeed appear mystical.

She raised her arms, in a gesture to encompass everyone in the room. 'Let us begin.'

For some moments there was absolute silence, as she appeared to enter a deep trance. Then, it may have been that I imagined it, an icy cold spread among us. Madam Myra spoke in a language that was unknown to me in a pleading entreaty that made me more aware of Holmes, whose stifled laughter had begun to escape him.

A frantic rapping began from beneath us.
'Welcome,' Madam Myra cried. 'Who is it that has joined our circle?'
'In my earthly form, I was Rose Traherne,' an echoing voice replied.

A woman stood up quickly from a seat near the front of the room. 'My Rose,' she wailed. 'How I miss you, my love.'

'Do not grieve for me, mother. All is good here, and I am happy.'

'Will you show yourself to us?' Madam Myra interrupted.

'It is permitted to cross the Divide, but briefly.' The words had hardly died away before a blue shape materialised above us. It shimmered like disturbed water and became the head and shoulders of a young girl.

Mrs Traherne was close to tears. 'Rose, is it really you? Are you with your father?'

The apparition hesitated, and then spoke for the last time before fading from our sight. 'Father is here. He is happy also and misses you. But I am being called. I must go now, mother.'

The figure had disappeared and Holmes seemed to be having difficulty breathing, as a ripple of astonished chatter broke out among the audience.

Mr Collins got to his feet, his huge frame looming in the semi-darkness, and appealed to Madam Myra. 'I beg of you, summon my departed wife, so that I can say the farewell that I was denied when she was taken from me.'

I sensed a change in Holmes. He was wondering, as was I, whether Mr Collins had been convinced by the demonstration or if his intention was to reveal the falseness of it.

Madam Myra considered. 'Very well,' she said at last, 'I will try to make contact.'

The hush returned, as Madam Myra again became still. After a moment her body shuddered, as if she were attempting to break loose from something that gripped her in a harsh embrace.

'She is coming,' she gasped. 'She is using me to speak to you.'

Mr Collins resumed his seat, his anticipation evident.

'My dear Fortesque,' Madam Myra said in a quite different voice. 'How sorry I was, that we were separated so soon.'

'Tell me again,' Mr Collins replied in a desperate croak, 'in that eloquent French you spoke so often, how much you cared for me.'

Madam Myra did not reply for long moments, and then the strange voice continued. 'There are no languages here, my love. I have no need of my former French, or of the one we shared. Only the tongue of compassion and tolerance is spoken. Do not despair, you will join me one day and....'

'Liar!' Mr Collins shouted loudly. Everyone turned towards him as he rose again. 'My wife knew no other language than that which was her native tongue.'

He ran headlong towards Madam Myra, and would have seized her by the throat had she not disappeared behind the curtain. As he searched frantically among its folds, Holmes raced past him to the corner of the room and disappeared.

Now total confusion surrounded me. Most of the others were aghast and had risen from their seats to move about aimlessly. Two women, one of them Mrs Traherne, were crying, while the men wore expressions of astonishment that their beliefs and hopes should be so shattered.

Sherlock Holmes reappeared, brushing aside the curtain and ushering Madam Myra, the midget and a girl of about twelve before him. Mr Collins looked on furiously.

'Allow me to introduce Mr and Mrs Marmion Kester, and their daughter Anna,' my friend began. 'Their profession is the operating of fraudulent exhibitions such as you have witnessed tonight, though they had not yet reached the point of demanding or begging for money.'

'And who are you, sir?' asked one of the men.

'My name is Sherlock Holmes. I am well versed in criminal activity, and this swindle was brought to my attention.'

'But how was it done?' the third woman, an obvious spinster, asked.

'Mrs Kester is adept at altering her voice, I would wager that her repertoire extends from a fishwife to a countess, and her daughter provided that of Miss Rose Traherne. The tapping from beneath the floor was the work of Mr Kester, using a broom-handle in the cellar. It was all rather unconvincing, and I confess to being disappointed.'

'But, the image?' A thin man, shy-looking and visibly shaken by the proceedings, asked in a trembling voice.

'That is easily explained,' Holmes replied. 'Suspended above our heads you will see a large mirror. It was lowered in the darkness, by means of a rope thrown over a beam. That was the screen to which the image was directed through the lenses of a device similar to that known as a "magic lantern", or by a technique which I believe is called "Pepper's Ghost".' He looked directly at me. 'We have come across this sort of trickery before, have we not, Watson?'

'Indeed, we have,' I replied.

Holmes then proceeded to interview each of the others in turn. When this was concluded, he took me aside. 'Mark these two points well, Watson: None of the others knew each other before tonight, and each received an identical letter to that of Mr Collins.'

The thin man who had asked about the spectral image approached. His fear was evident, for he trembled visibly.

On impulse, I asked. 'Are you ill, sir?'

He cringed before me. 'My nerves are in shreds. It is an affliction I constantly suffer from.'

It was difficult to imagine how he earned his living in such a permanently excited state, and I confess to yielding to my curiosity. 'Pray, what is your profession?'

'I am an architect.' He produced a card of the London Association, as if he felt he needed to prove his statement. His teeth chattered as he continued, looking first at me, and then at Holmes. 'This appalling assault on the sentiments of those of us who came here to remember our loved and dearest is too much for me. I would like to leave now, if there is no objection.'

'Very well,' Holmes agreed. 'You may all depart. But pray do not do so before furnishing your names and where you are to be found to my associate, Dr Watson. I will see that things take their proper course. '

With much murmuring they prepared to file out of the room, after the key had been retrieved from Marmion Kester. Only one person paused: Mr Collins thanked Holmes and myself profusely and shook our hands.

'There is something more,' Holmes called as they gathered near the doorway. 'Some of you, on returning to your homes, may find that intruders have broken in during your absence. If that has occurred, I ask that you immediately contact me by telegraph at Baker Street and notify Scotland Yard also.'

There was a nodding of heads and murmurs of assent, as they left.

On Holmes' instruction, I locked the door again. He faced our prisoners, his expression stern.

'I really think that you could have done better, Mr Kester,' he began. 'There is really no excuse, for you have operated this and similar contemptible deceptions for some years.'

'You recognised me. I felt it in my bones.' The midget said hopelessly.

Holmes nodded. 'I knew that you were likely behind this before I entered the hotel, and the sight of you was confirmation. You are not unknown at Scotland Yard, by reputation, though you have not been caught until now.'

'What will happen to us?' Mrs Kester asked in a shaky voice.

'Prison, of course.' Holmes shrugged and waited while they absorbed the probability. 'There is, however, a single alternative.'

The midget's eyes widened, and a faint hope lightened his wife's expression. Their daughter seemed about to weep.

'For your daughter's sake,' my friend continued, 'I will give you two hours start before I inform Inspector Lestrade. If you leave here directly for Paddington, to catch the next express from the capital, you will have a fair chance. I advise you, Mr Kester, to seek honest work and to pursue an honourable life, in order that your family may not suffer.'

'And in exchange?' Kester asked, not meeting our eyes.

'What I have just described is entirely dependent on your explanation. You must tell me how your performance of tonight was arranged. Be specific and leave nothing out, and you may all walk from this room free.'

'I will tell you all that I know,' the midget said with an anxious expression. 'I had a strange visitor, one night about a week ago. He stood at my door and would not enter the house. I later realised that this was probably because he wished to remain in the darkness so as not to be identified. He was a tall man, but stout, wearing a long coat and a broad-brimmed hat pulled low down. I could see that he had a long red scar on his face, and a full beard.'

Holmes nodded. 'And what was the purpose of the visit?'

'He seemed to know all about my business,' the little man continued. 'He gave me fifty pounds and told me that I must attend here tonight to conduct a séance. He said that all arrangements had been made and I must not fail him, and from his manner I felt bullied and unable to refuse.'

'You resented him. That is why tonight's performance was, shall we say, sparse?'

'No man works well, or takes more trouble than he has to, when he is threatened.'

'Wisely said. Is there anything more that you can tell me?'

'One thing only, Mr Holmes.'

'What is it, pray?'

'The last thing that this man said, before he walked away into the night, was that I must not think of leaving the district without fulfilling my obligation. He assured me that if I attempted to do so, then my family, my loved and dearest, as he referred to them, would be killed, most slowly and painfully.'

#

Holmes was unusually quiet next morning, over breakfast. His monosyllabic answers to my attempts to start a conversation suggested that he was giving much thought to our present problem, and so I desisted and ate my bacon and eggs in silence.

This changed abruptly when Mrs Hudson cleared away the plates. No sooner had the door closed after her than my friend became suddenly animated, beginning his observations, conclusions and questions from the moment we sat down.

'There is more to this, Watson,' he began as he settled into his armchair. 'I cannot see why this mysterious caller of Mr Kester's went to the trouble of arranging that farce last night.'

'Nor I. It cannot have been to lure the participants from their homes, since we have received no notifications of burglary or anything else.'

'And why, particularly, this group? There has to be a common thread running through the lives of each of them, but my interviews yielded no such thing.'

'You mentioned, I think, that they were previously unknown to each other, and had each received the same summons?'

Holmes sat back in his chair. 'Indeed. Pray read aloud the notes you made of each person, omitting their addresses but including their names, professions, and your impressions.'

I hurriedly retrieved my notebook from my pocket, noticing that Holmes had closed his eyes and adopted a meditative posture.

'Mr Fortescue Collins,' I began, 'our client. We have discussed him before, so I assume you have already reached your conclusions?'

Holmes gave an almost imperceptible nod.

'Then we have Mrs Susan Traherne, the widow whose daughter was 'brought back' by Madam Myra. She struck me as a most distressed woman, who will be no better for her experience. Mrs Olivia Burton is also a widow, since her husband died at Maiwand.'

'A comrade of yours, perhaps?'

'No, I never knew him. Mrs Burton was a reticent woman, reluctant to speak of what she had witnessed. Miss Adeline Murrell is an unmarried shop assistant. She complained constantly, saying that she had expected to be reunited with her mother for a few minutes but was bitterly disappointed.'

'That leaves two gentlemen I think, doctor.'

I nodded, although Holmes was unable to see me. 'The first is Mr Godfrey Franklin, a butcher. He is a muscular, red-faced man who I suspect is normally of a jovial disposition despite the cruel line of his mouth but, as the opportunity to speak to his departed infant son did not present itself, last night exhibited symptoms of melancholia.'

'And the other?'

Mr Carlton Woodchester, whom we spoke to. He is an architect by trade and suffers from an extreme nervous condition. As you will remember, he is tall and thin with a slight stoop to his frame. I noticed also that his eyes are ice-blue, with a look which I would have interpreted as compassionless, had I not recognised it as caused by his ailment.'

'Thank you, Watson. Your observations are most informative. There is something troubling me about a remark I heard during our conversations of last night. The words should have meant something to me, but I cannot bring them to mind.'

'Was it something that the midget said?'

'Perhaps. It will come to me, presently.'

A thought occurred to me. 'Holmes, you asked everyone at the séance to send a wire if they were burgled.'

'Quite so, but it came to nothing.'

'You thought the séance could be a ploy to get those people away from their homes?'

'We have met that device before, on at least two occasions.'

'That is true. But what if, this time, the object of the séance was to gather these men and women together?'

Sherlock Holmes sat very still, and then he clapped a hand to his forehead. 'Watson, how many times have I said that it is you who should be the detective, rather than I? My dear fellow, how often you see things that I fail to perceive.'

Hiding my embarrassment, I said that I was glad to have been of help.

'As you always are, dear friend.'

To glimpse beneath that cold and logical mask for an instant, when the warm heart beneath shows clearly through, is to see a different Holmes revealed. Perhaps, I thought, this truly is the essence of the man.

Holmes rushed to the bookshelf and took down his index. For the next few minutes he whipped through its pages of newspaper cuttings while on his hands and knees. Finally, he gave as cry of triumph.

'Aha! I knew it, Watson. My memory has not yet begun to fail me. I now know the identity of Mr Kester's visitor, the man who arranged last night's proceedings.' He jumped to his feet and seized his hat and coat. 'But before we can proceed, I must seek confirmation at Scotland Yard. I do hope that Lestrade is in attendance today. Please tell Mrs Hudson to expect me after luncheon.'

With that, before I was able to reply or comment, he left.

#

I occupied myself until lunch time with writing up notes from my practice, in preparation for visiting several patients within the next few days. Mrs Hudson appeared briefly, bearing beef sandwiches and coffee, but I was otherwise left to my own devices.

It was almost three o'clock before Holmes returned. I heard his rapid steps upon the stairs and concluded that he was in a state of excitement. Before he entered, I heard him shout to our good landlady for a fresh pot of coffee.

'This case is rapidly gaining speed, Watson,' he called as he flung the door shut behind him. 'It is no longer the trivial affair that began with the séance, but a saga of multiple murder!'

'Good heavens!' I retorted. 'What did you learn at Scotland Yard?'

'I will tell you when I have consumed some refreshment. Ah, thank you, Mrs Hudson, this will be sufficient to sustain me until dinner, I think.'

That good lady left the tray on a side table and withdrew, critical as always of Holmes' missing his meals as he often did while concerned with a case.

My friend drank two cups of the steaming liquid, then poured a third from the pot but left it to cool.

'It has not been publicly announced in order to avoid panic,' he began, 'but London has suffered a veritable epidemic of murder recently.'

'Is there some maniac at large, then?'

'I think not. I see it all as a carefully planned trail of revenge. I have established a connection, with the aid of Lestrade and the official files, between five victims as of yesterday. A further two, who might well have attended the séance last night had they a mind to, were killed in the early hours of this morning. Mr Jonathan Dermott, a builder, and Mrs Rebecca Laversham, the widow of a vicar, were strangled in their beds.'

'This is appalling!'

'Indeed. However, I am quite certain that we were in the company of the murderer at the séance, and that we can exclude the women that were present from our suspicions.'

'He was there?' I said, astonished. 'Why are you so certain that the killer is not a woman, Holmes? We have encountered many who are more than capable, before now.'

He picked up his coffee cup. 'There is another in the pot, doctor, if you would like it. No? Well, I suppose it will have cooled somewhat, by now. If the murderer of the previous five victims is the same as the slayer of the two this morning, then it must be a man. One of the five, a very heavily built fellow, was manhandled as high as the railings across Westminster Bridge, and then pushed over into the Thames. It is unlikely that a woman, even one of exceptional power and condition, could have summoned such strength.'

'Also,' I ventured, 'it was a man who ordered Mr Kester, under threat, to arrange the séance. Assuming, of course, that he and the murderer are the same person.'

'They are, Watson, there can be no other explanation. Nevertheless, Mr Kester's observation alone is not conclusive. Remember the visitor's appearance: a full beard, a scarred face, a hat pulled down over the eyes - a classic disguise.'

'He also described him as "stout", and none of the women we encountered last night were excessively so.'

Holmes drained his cup and replaced it on the tray. 'That is true, but again it is not conclusive. A little padding, correctly placed, and a slight person becomes a heavy one. I considered that our killer might have used a female accomplice for the visit, but there is no evidence to suggest it.'

'What will you do now, Holmes?'

'I suggest a walk, perhaps in St James Park. On the way I have a couple of wires to send and an arrangement to make. By then it will be time for dinner, and I think we can forego Mrs Hudson's cheese and potato pie until tomorrow, in favour of Simpson's-in-the-Strand. When our appetites are satisfied, we can proceed to the final act of this drama, if things have gone well.'

Shortly after, we caught a hansom to Charing Cross where Holmes sent his wires from the Post Office, and then to a two-storey building at the far end of Long Acre. Here he had told me he was certain to be able to hire a room that he had used before. The swarthy-looking man who answered the door as I waited in the carriage seemed pleased to see my friend and handed him a key. I assumed that this was someone from one of my friend's past cases, like so many of his acquaintances about whom, I hoped, he would tell me one day.

St James Park was a pleasant place to be, on a late afternoon such as this. The strolling couples and the occasional gentleman alone wandered among the fresh blooms, as did a considerable number of nannies wearing bonnets as they trundled their charges along in perambulators. The smell of new-mown grass was refreshing to the soul and Holmes, in excellent spirits, talked of many things.

At precisely six o'clock, he broke off suddenly. 'Could you manage dinner yet, Watson?'

'I believe I could do justice to it.'

'And I. Simpson's is a short walk from here.'

We found ourselves in the panelled dining room a short while later. Situated at street level we were, as Holmes put it, 'always safe from feminine intrusion here'. The tablecloths and napkins were of the crispest white linen, as were the spotless aprons of the waiters, and the low hum of conversation most civilized. The food was superb, and even my friend was in appreciation of it as he ate with unusual gusto.

'Come Watson,' he consulted his pocket watch as we finished our glasses of an excellent brandy, 'it is time. We go to apprehend a callous murderer, for the hangman.'

We arrived back at the building in Long Acre soon after. Holmes let us in with the key he had been given, and we ascended a flight of dusty stairs at the end of a long corridor. The room contained nothing more than a table and four chairs and was in need of some decoration, but my friend pronounced it ideal for our purpose after glancing down from the wide window into the street. He opened the window halfway, presumably to dispel a slightly musty smell, and I noticed a cobweb or two hanging from the ceiling. I did not care for this place, but Holmes had assured me that we would not be here for long.

Again, he consulted his pocket watch. 'It is time for the first of our visitors to arrive I think, Watson. Ah, I see him across the street.'

Moments later we heard a heavy tread upon the stairs, ascending quickly after an initial hesitation. The door creaked open to admit one of the men who had attended the séance. I saw that it was Mr Godfrey Franklin, the butcher.

'What is the meaning of summoning me so urgently, Mr Holmes?' He demanded, slightly breathless from his climb. 'I have a business to run, and cannot just walk away like this.' Again, I noted the cruel line of the man's mouth, and the intimidating stance of that strong body.

'Pray calm yourself, my dear fellow,' Holmes replied. 'It is no understatement to say that being here may save your life. If you will watch the street, Watson, and call me if you see anything of significance, I would be grateful.'

With that he ushered Mr Franklin out onto the landing, closing the door behind them. I did not know what I was expected to report, but I looked down through the window at the evening traffic while straining my ears to catch anything from their conversation.

At first, I heard a cry of outrage from Mr Franklin, and I wondered if this was some trap of Holmes' to prove him to be the man we sought. The exchange became muted, but quick, with Mr Franklin's protests becoming more emphatic and Holmes' quiet tones increasingly insistent. Finally, I heard resignation creep into our visitor's voice, and wondered if my friend had secured a confession.

'Mr Woodchester is about to join us,' I remarked as they re-entered the room.

'Excellent,' Holmes stopped to listen to the footfalls on the stairs. 'And twenty minutes exactly after Mr Franklin, the time I requested.'

Mr Woodchester came in, the hand holding his stick shaking noticeably. His body trembled as he looked enquiringly at all three of us in turn.

'Gentlemen, I received a telegram earlier, asking me to come here on a matter of life and death. Mr Holmes, what is happening?'

'I have received information from Scotland Yard,' Holmes announced. 'It was to the effect that a murderer is at large who they have been unable to identify. It is only a matter of time however, for they have discovered a connection with the séance which we all attended last night. It is suspected that everyone who attended is in mortal danger, and so all are being temporarily taken into police custody for their own protection. I recommend that both you gentlemen accompany Inspector Lestrade, who will arrive here very soon before seeking out the remaining potential victims.'

'This is outrageous!' Mr Franklin retorted, his face reddening. 'I am no criminal!'

Mr Woodchester gave us all a long slow look, his ice-blue eyes revealing nothing. 'Yes,' he said in his wavering voice, 'we must be protected while there is danger. One cannot know how long such a man has, to finish his task. He may feel compelled to strike again before he can be apprehended. Thank you, Mr Holmes, for the timely warning.' He turned to Franklin. 'Come, sir, we will meet the police agent in the street. The killer would not dare to reveal himself with so many passers-by to witness his act.' At the top of the stairs he said over his shoulder: 'Goodbye to you gentlemen. I doubt that we will meet again.'

Holmes, with his head held to one side, listened as they descended. He seemed to be taking account of the sounds until they ceased at the foot of the stairs, when he cried suddenly: 'Quickly, Watson. That man entrusted his life to me. I cannot fail him!'

We reached the corridor in time to see Mr Woodchester take a step away from his companion, at the same time drawing a short sword from the casing of his stick. Raising it above his head he prepared to plunge it into the back of Mr Franklin, who had only just become aware of the sudden change in his companion's pace. It seemed that nothing could prevent the murderer claiming another victim, when a door on either side of the passage was flung open and two burly constables appeared.

Mr Franklin was guided safely out of range but Mr Woodchester, seeing that he was caught in a trap, pierced the arm of one of the constables and, with strength that I would never have suspected, threw off the other. His weapon fell to the floor as he ran headlong for the door and out into the street. To my surprise, Holmes restrained me from pursuit.

'No, Watson, this way. Back up the stairs, as fast as you can.'

We climbed quickly, Holmes drawing me to the half-open window as we reached the room. Among the crowd, I saw that uniformed officers were converging on the building from both directions.

'Observe the fate of one of the most callous killers that I have known,' he said as we looked down.

A cab departed from the entrance, the horse racing.

'Holmes!' I cried. 'He is getting away!'

'I hardly think so, old fellow,' he replied calmly. 'The coachman is Inspector Lestrade.'

We watched as a police wagon entered the street and followed the cab. Then another appeared to block its progress. Caught between the two the cab came to a rapid halt and Lestrade, with his prisoner now safely away from the passers-by, jumped down and opened the door. I thought that moment would mark the capture of this man who had slain so many for reasons I did not yet know, but this was not to be. The door on the opposite side of the cab was hurled back and a thin figure leapt blindly into the path of a four-wheeler speeding from the other direction. A terrible cry that turned the head of every person in the street ripped through the air, as the body became somehow entangled and was dragged along the road surface. By the time the driver had brought the four-wheeler to rest, all that remained was a long dark smudge of blood and a lump of mangled flesh and clothing. Several ladies fell in a dead faint and had to be supported by their escorts, and other men became suddenly, unexpectedly, ill.

I turned away with my mind reeling from the horror, back into the room where Holmes had retreated, unmoved.

'Justice will not be denied,' he observed without emotion, 'but I fear that she has robbed the hangman of his work this day.'

#

Midnight had long passed, by the time we found ourselves once more in Baker Street. We sank into our armchairs and Holmes poured us each a glass of brandy. We knew that what remained of this night held little sleep for either of us.

I sipped my drink before placing my glass on a side table. 'I confess to being all at sea with this affair,' I told him.

'When you called Mr Franklin to that room in Long Acre, I fully expected an arrest.'

A faint smile crossed my friend's face as he lit his cherrywood pipe. 'In fact, I was quite in the dark myself from the outset, until my index confirmed something that I had been trying to remember. After the additional information that Lestrade was kind enough to furnish from the official files, I became quite certain of the true nature of the case.'

'You mentioned that vengeance was involved, I recall. I have seen a glimmer of light shining through all that has happened since last night, or rather the night before, but the complete picture eludes me.'

'Very well, Watson,' Holmes blew out a long stream of smoke and rested his head against the back of his chair, closing his eyes. 'Take up your notebook and I will endeavour to tell the story, as it revealed itself to me, from the beginning. However, much as I am sorry to disappoint you, there are certain hidden implications here that compel me to forbid publication of these events for ten years at least. Doubtlessly the public will be no less eager to read your efforts, when they are finally set before them.'

At once I shrugged off the weariness that had been creeping over me, and turned my notebook to a fresh page. 'I am ready, Holmes.'

'Please limit your interruptions to a minimum.'

I held my pencil ready and, when he had taken a moment to arrange his thoughts, he told me all he had discovered.

'This case really begins at the Old Bailey, ten years ago. It was then that Nathaniel Jervis, the real name of our Mr Woodchester, received a heavy sentence for his part in a plot to rob the Bank of England. You see, Watson, his claim to be an architect was quite genuine, and he used his knowledge to instruct the thieves on how to enter the premises secretly, using the plans which had been made available to him by the firm with which he held a position of trust. Jervis accepted his fate philosophically at first but showing neither remorse nor fear. His prison life was uneventful, until two things changed everything. First, he contracted a nervous disease which worsened progressively, and then his wife, who he apparently loved dearly, died of consumption from the occupation she had been forced to take up. Jervis became a bitter man, furiously seeking revenge upon the world. The judge who sentenced him had died since his incarceration, as had all but two of the jurors. You will recall their names: Jonathan Dermott and Mrs Rebecca Laversham.'

'The two latest victims,' I remembered.

'Precisely. Apparently, it took Jervis longer to find them, than the others.'

'But Holmes,' I risked another intrusion, 'if everyone concerned with the trial is deceased, what connection have the other victims? I think you mentioned five others.'

'That was the question I could not answer, at first. I was slow, which proves that I have much to learn, even now. When Mr Kester related the incident of the visitor who caused the séance to be arranged, he stated that a phrase was used regarding his family: the unknown man threatened Kester's "loved and dearest". That struck me as an unusual or peculiar phrase - you or I would most probably say: "nearest and dearest", or something similar, since that is a common expression. Yet I knew that I had heard those words before. When I consulted my index, I came across a newspaper cutting about Jervis' trial, and read that he had used the same phrase in the hearing of a *Standard* reporter covering the proceedings. Later, when I remembered that I had heard it yet again from the mouth of Mr Woodchester, the identity of our murderer became a certainty, although I had no proof such as a court would accept.'

He fell silent as he puffed at his pipe and I heard a cab rattle down Baker Street, no doubt transporting an all-night reveller back to his home. The gas jet spurted loudly, causing Holmes to open his eyes momentarily before resuming his previous posture.

'That is the background to this case and my method of identifying the perpetrator. Jervis was released about two months ago and set about finding his victims at once. This is where that expression of his takes on a new meaning - his intention became, since ten of the jurors were beyond his vengeance, to inflict their intended fate upon the nearest living relative of each of them. His reason had deserted him, to be replaced, I would say, by the bitterness that had engulfed his heart.'

'Such an attitude of mind is easily tipped into madness. God knows, I have seen this before.'

Holmes nodded. 'It was thus explained why none of the intended victims at the séance had any previous knowledge of each other. He traced the first five relatives and despatched them in various ways: some were poisoned or strangled, one run down in the street by an unmarked coach. During his extensive enquiries in seeking out his victims, Jervis came to learn much about them. He was devising methods to encounter and dispose of each when it struck him that here was a common denominator - the eight that were left had each suffered bereavement, within the last few years. That was how the visit to Kester, who was a trickster he probably heard about while in prison, came about. With his body padded and heavily disguised, Jervis threatened the midget and paid him to arrange the gathering, appealing to the heartfelt sensibilities of those attending. As you know, they were made up of widows and some who had lost their marriage mates or children, all of which Jervis gambled would seize the prospect of a reunion, however unlikely or temporary. The exceptions, of course, were the two original jurors who were older and wiser. They refused to have anything to do with what they saw as an un-Biblical ceremony and were in consequence dealt with soon after.'

'But I still cannot see what Jervis sought to achieve from the séance.'

Holmes knocked out his pipe on the hearth. 'Here I must, with regret, introduce some conjecture. Jervis must have had some method of destroying the entire assembly. I have theorized that it could have been by the use of explosives. None were found so perhaps it was planned for a subsequent gathering, if such an arrangement proved to be a possibility. However, I am convinced that he abandoned that plan because you and I were in attendance and he recognised us - the prospect of being caught before his revenge was complete was intolerable to him.'

'So, he killed the first five relatives of the jurors and then, after the séance, the two original jurors from the trial, and his intention was to murder the six at the séance, also?'

'That would have completed his vengeance.'

'But that is thirteen, Holmes. A jury is composed of twelve.'

'Which is how I came to realise, when the true situation lay before me, that the murderer had been among us at the séance.'

I considered, as Holmes looked increasingly weary, all that I had heard.

'There is only one thing more, that I have not understood.'

'And what is that, pray?' He asked, stifling a yawn.

'Why did you argue with Mr Franklin, just before Woodchester, or Jervis, arrived earlier?'

'At that time, I still had no actual proof of Jervis' guilt. I requested Mr Franklin's help in a matter of life and death, but he agreed only when I explained that it could be *his* life in jeopardy.'

'To be fair to the man, Holmes, he was almost killed by Jervis.'

'He was in little danger, providing that the constables followed my instructions and acted quickly enough. In any case, old fellow, if Franklin had refused and Jervis had gone free, it would have placed five other lives in jeopardy.'

'I suppose, in his unbalanced state, he could have claimed more, unrelated, victims, also.'

'It was my intention to prevent any such occurrences.'

'I think we can confidently be assured that you succeeded.'

'Quite so.' Holmes got to his feet. 'Well, doctor, now that I have related this pretty tale for your archives, I propose to retire without further delay. I suggest you place your notes in a safe place and resolve to retrieve them at some future time. When you have done that, I recommend that you follow my example.'

The Adventure of the Moonlit Shadow

As my long association with my friend Mr Sherlock Holmes progressed, we shared many adventures of an unusual nature. Most were brought to a satisfactory conclusion, but there remained some with aspects that were beyond explanation. It is one of these that I propose to relate here.

The first light of a late November day was settling on the city as I let myself into our lodgings in Baker Street. Tiredness lay heavily upon me, but I considered the loss of a night's sleep a small price to pay - I had remained at the side of my patient until his fever had at last begun to subside. I reached the top of the stairs having made little noise, I did not wish to disturb Holmes who was usually a late riser. I opened the door carefully. I quickly saw that such precautions were unnecessary, for he sat fully dressed at the breakfast table and apparently in good spirits.

'Watson, my dear fellow!' he cried. 'Do come and join me. I see that you are in need of sleep, but a good serving of Mrs Hudson's bacon and eggs will fortify you first.'

I took off my hat and coat and sat opposite him. 'You are up unusually early, Holmes.'

'Much to the contrary,' he said after he had called out to our landlady. 'I have not been to bed.'

'You caught Nicholls on one of his night raids, then?'

'Indeed we did. I had deduced his intentions correctly. He was captured in the act of breaking into a jeweller's premises in Hammersmith, and Gregson now has him behind bars.'

'And so,' I observed as Mrs Hudson laid my breakfast before me, 'we have both had our successes.'

He nodded his head but said no more, and watched in silence as I ate. While we awaited our coffee, he began to open a pile of letters which he had paid no attention to until now.

'The late post from yesterday,' he explained. 'I had left before it arrived.'

'One envelope has a coat-of-arms,' I pointed out.

Holmes raised his eyebrows and used his breakfast knife as a letter-opener. His hawk-like expression changed as he read the document.

'What do you make of this, Watson?'

I took it from him and read the few words, which were written in an ornate script.

I have proof at last, and it is indisputable.
But there is little time.
I beg you to come at your first convenience. Bring
Lestrade if you can.
Trentlemere.

'From someone of your previous acquaintance, obviously,' I deduced. 'Also, he knows Lestrade.'

'Indeed. Lord Trentlemere has cause to remember us both.'

'I cannot recall such a case.'

'That is hardly surprising. You and I saw little of each other for a while, following your marriage. The Edmund

Saunders affair took place during that time.'

I nodded. 'That name is familiar to me.'

'The newspapers made much of it, but the fact remains - Saunders is a murderer who escaped the rope.' Holmes frown deepened. 'But perhaps not for much longer.'

'This letter then, refers to new evidence that has been discovered?'

'Apparently, but that remains to be seen. Lord Trentlemere's obsession with proving Saunders' guilt has been unceasing, over the years.'

'Will you tell me about the case, Holmes?' I asked, unable to contain my curiosity.

He leaned back in his chair with a look in his eyes that I have rarely seen - remembering an unsuccessful case.

'Lord Trentlemere is among the kindest and most courteous men that it has ever been my good fortune to meet,' he began. 'Yet his reaction was hostile at the outset when his daughter, Leone, was courted by Edmund Saunders. At first, his Lordship told me, it was no more than instinct. He felt that something about the young man was not genuine. Secretly, he employed agents to explore Saunders' background. Their findings were that his claims of family connections and wealth were false, as were those of leading an honest life.'

'The man was a criminal?'

'He was, and is. He demonstrated it in the extreme when, having been convinced by her father's evidence, Leone faced him with it and told him that their courtship was at an end. Her strangled body was found in a country lane, shortly after.'

'That is appalling. Was Saunders arrested?'

'Of course,' Holmes said thoughtfully.

'Lestrade went to Norfolk to investigate and make the arrest, only to find that there was no substantial evidence. Saunders had friends who swore that he was in their company at the time the murder was said to have taken place. Scotland Yard could discover no proof, and that was when Lord Trentlemere called me in. Much to my everlasting regret, I could offer no assistance. Saunders is one of the most careful and vicious villains I have come across. Both his Lordship and myself were convinced of his guilt, indeed he all but admitted it with his insults and taunts, but nothing that would stand up in a courtroom ever came to light. Since then, Saunders has been suspected of several robberies and another murder, but still he has escaped the net.'

I shook my head. 'Intelligence and evil are a combination forged in hell.'

'As you say, Watson. For a time, Lord Trentlemere was a broken man, but the flame of revenge burned within him. He swore that Saunders would hang and devoted himself to bringing this about. Paid agents, and his Lordship himself, buried themselves in an intense examination of Saunders' life, with the object of discovering any incriminating aspect. Until now this has met with no success, and Lord Trentlemere occasionally receives anonymous and taunting letters, as do I, to ensure that we do not forget Saunders' triumphs over the law.'

'This is monstrous, Holmes! The man's impudence is intolerable.'

'I am sure his Lordship would agree with you. However, it seems that he has accomplished his purpose, and wishes me to verify it. I can only hope that, as the letter says, there is no mistake.'

'So you will go to Norfolk. Doubtlessly, Lestrade will accompany you.'

Holmes shook his head. 'Lestrade is away on a case in Brighton.'

'Then, if you will have me, I will take his place.'

'Watson, you are exhausted. You must rest.'

'I will wash my face in cold water,' I said as I stood up, 'and put on a clean collar. After that, I am at your disposal.'

As I made my way to my room, Holmes was already reaching for his Bradshaw.

#

It had begun to rain heavily as we left Baker Street. Now, as our train steamed from Liverpool Street Station into open countryside, the sky grew ever darker.

'Why do you suppose Lord Trentlemere's letter was written with such urgency, Holmes?' I asked. 'After all, he has patiently studied Saunders' activities for several years.'

He turned away from the window. 'The phrase, "there is little time" struck me at once. Probably he is ill, for his health was never good.'

'One wonders then why he did not summon you by means of a telegram, which would have reached you more quickly.'

'Lord Trentlemere has his peculiarities, like most men. He never sends telegrams because he believes there is a lack of privacy there. The telegraphist, you see, is aware of the contents even before the message is sent. Also, Lord Trentlemere's estate is some distance from the nearest Post

Office.'

I nodded my acknowledgement, and there was silence between us for a while. Sometime after mid-day we made our way to the dining coach where an excellent steak-and-kidney pie was served, and on our return to our reserved smoker the incessant beat of the wheels against the tracks quickly lulled me into sleep.

#

'How long have I slept, Holmes?' I asked as I awoke.

He stared through the window still, as if he had not moved since returning from our luncheon, at the driving rain and the near-darkness.

'Four hours and ten minutes. I trust you feel refreshed.'

'Yes, but I must apologise. I have been poor company.'

'You were in need of rest, and I have done much thinking during the time. The conductor called out a few moments ago - in ten minutes we will arrive in Norwich.'

As we approached the station I caught a glimpse of the Foundry Bridge, which spans the River Wensum. The train slowed and came to a halt, and we stepped out to be confronted by the long red brick and stucco station building. People moved about in droves, shaking soaked umbrellas and huddled in rain-capes as they found shelter beneath the ironwork and glass concourse.

Holmes stopped to study a timetable affixed to the waiting room wall. 'This way, Watson,' he said after a moment. 'We must catch the local train to Queen's Mount.'

We purchased further tickets and were soon settled in a much smaller train that rattled away down a branch line in response to a quick whistle-blast. The darkness was total now, and the rain more fierce than ever.

'What station are we bound for, Holmes?' I asked my friend. He produced his tobacco pouch and his old briar, which he began to fill.

'Little Tensdale is the nearest to Lord Trentlemere's estate, if my memory serves me well. It is no more than five miles distant.'

Indeed, Holmes had only just finished his pipe and I a cigarette, before we alighted at a small country station. A single gas lamp shone above the door of the station master's office where two men, one in uniform, stood deep in conversation. As we approached the train belched out a cloud of steam, before setting off backwards in the direction of its arrival.

'Good evening,' Holmes began. 'Would you be kind enough to tell me where we can hire a trap?'

The station master straightened his uniform jacket, and they both turned to face us. 'Not here, at this time of night, sir. Where was it you were wanting to go?'

'We are making for Lord Trentlemere's estate, but if there is no transportation available perhaps you could direct us to a hotel?'

The station master rubbed his unshaven jaw. 'The Fox and Feather should be able to put you up for the night. It is, I would say, no more than half a mile from here. What d'you say, Tom?'

The other man knocked out his pipe and smiled. 'I think we can do these gentlemen better. I have to pass the estate on my way home to Little Tensdale, and I can let them off by the side entrance. That is if they don't mind getting wet in an open cart?'

Holmes assured him that we did not, whereupon he produced and put on a seaman's oilskin and led us to an overhanging clump of trees opposite the station. The horse tethered beneath stamped his hooves as if impatient to be away, and Holmes and I scrambled into the cart. Tom climbed aboard and glanced back once and, seemingly satisfied that we were adequately seated, shook the reins. The horse set off at once, at a brisk pace. Holmes and I wrapped our coats tightly around us and pulled our hats further down onto our heads.

In a short while we found ourselves on a dark and uneven country track, with the sinister shapes of bare trees on either side. In the distance a rumble of thunder warned of worse weather to come. I was able to make out the beginnings of a tall fence to our left, which continued until Tom drew the cart to a halt. 'There it is, sirs. You see the gap in the fence? If you go through there, there's a field to cross and then a bridge over the stream, after that you climb the hill and you're in front of Trentlemere Hall. The only other way, from here, is to the far right along the edge of the forest. There's a stile, but it's a treacherous path.'

We jumped down from the cart. Tom touched his cap and thanked Holmes for the coins that were pushed into his hand. He wished us well and continued on his way. No more than a few moments passed before he was lost in the darkness, with the sound of the horse's hooves growing steadily less distinct. After passing through the fence we could see, faintly, that a narrow path had been worn across the sodden field. Gusts of wind blew the long grass against our legs like whips, but we both wore stout walking boots and were able to make our way forward.

'Stay close to me, Watson,' Holmes said. 'In this darkness we could lose our way, or each other.'

Certainly there was not the faintest light to be seen, and any attempt to use a dark lantern would have been immediately foiled by the wind. Tom had indicated that a straight course would take us to the bridge, and we endeavoured not to waver and trudged on for perhaps half an hour. Finally, we reached a great oak, and we could see a darker line among the blackness which we took to be the first trees of the forest.

'There!' My friend exclaimed, and at the same moment I heard the roaring of the swollen stream.

I followed Holmes to where the land began to rise, just ahead.

It was then that something fantastical, something which I have never been able to explain satisfactorily, even to myself, occurred!

Another clap of thunder was followed by a streak of lightning which lit up everything around us. Holmes' long strides had taken him a little ahead of me, and between us a man appeared with his arms held up in warning. I had but a momentary glimpse of him, before he was gone.

'Holmes!' I cried. 'Stop at once!'

My friend obeyed, and in the darkness, I fancied he smiled. 'How did you know, Watson?'

'Know what, pray?'

'Look before you.'

I leaned to glance ahead. Another step would have taken us into the dark chasm left by the shattered bridge. The waters had risen to the extent that part of the structure had been carried away, while the remainder hung precariously from the opposite bank. The stream had become a raging torrent.

'How did you know?' Holmes repeated.

'A man came out of the darkness and warned us. You must have seen him.'

'I saw no one. Yet the warning was a timely one. Where is he now?'

I looked all around us. 'In this weather, and without light, I cannot tell.'

'The only sheltering-place is the oak we passed, and that is too far away. Could you have imagined our benefactor?'

'I think not. He was so near I could have touched him.'

Holmes murmured that I should squat down. I did so and he did the same, forming a shelter between us for the vesper that he produced from his coat. In its flare I saw my friend's puzzled expression, and I became similarly mystified as I realised his intention. He moved the flame over and around the patch of mud where the man had stood. There was no impression, no footprints - the surface was completely unmarked. He shook the vesper out, and I sensed that he looked at me critically.

'Doubtlessly it was the lightning, old fellow. It is easy to see what is not there, when the eyes are confused by such a brilliant flash.'

'But Holmes, I could have sworn!'

'Hallucination, nothing more. I am told they can be very convincing.'

'I suppose it must have been,' I said, feeling rather foolish.

'Now we must proceed along the edge of the forest. You will recall that Tom mentioned that it is an alternative route.'

As we moved towards the trees the cloud cleared suddenly, allowing a shaft of moonlight to pierce the darkness and aid our progress. The ground was uneven in places, and we sometimes stumbled as the downpour, a little lessened now, beat against us.

'I see it,' said Holmes, after we had travelled about half a mile. 'The stile is beyond that bent pine.'

This proved to be the case, and we entered the forest at that point. At once we found ourselves in a place of silence, a quiet that was broken only by the rain dripping from the branches. Moonlight shone onto the forest floor in patches where the branches above grew less thickly, lending a spectral glow to every clearing.

'Tread carefully,' my friend advised, 'there are thick roots underfoot.'

And so we continued, endeavouring to maintain a straight course to emerge within sight of Trentlemere Hall. We trod through saturated leaves and gnarled twigs for a while, before approaching a fork in the path.

Holmes stood still, his thin figure barely visible, deciding which direction we should pursue. Then to my absolute amazement I saw the vision of the man that I had imagined earlier appear again before us. He stood in a pool of moonlight, pointing along the right fork and meeting my astonished gaze with a stern stare. He vanished in an instant and this time I said nothing for fear that Holmes would begin to doubt my sanity. I had thought that he had seen nothing, but as always, he had seen more than I.

'It was a moonlit shadow Watson, nothing more. Such a patch of light amid this dense darkness causes our eyes to play us false. Come, old fellow, let us take the right fork, for that seems to me the most likely way out of here. Take care!'

I was greatly relieved to be spared an argument with Holmes, for the apparition had saved us before and for some reason I felt it would not have failed to do so again. A few minutes later an overhead thunderclap preceded a sudden lightning strike which immediately brought down a heavy branch. In the poor light I could see that it was large enough to have crushed us, and that it had fallen upon the left fork where we had stood a few minutes before.

'We seem to have had our share of luck this evening,' was his only comment.

Nor was that the end of the strangeness of that night. Careful to return to the same course, we avoided several thick groups of trees that obstructed us. This took us some time, but on emerging I saw that the trees ahead were thinning, and that the night sky was visible a short distance beyond.

Once more, the apparition stood in our path, holding up a hand and pointing to the flooded earth with the other. Holmes made no sign that he had seen anything out of the ordinary but he too, studied the forest floor.

'We have seen this before, Watson,' he said. 'You will recall the lair of Stapleton, on Dartmoor.'

With that he lifted a thick, dead branch from among the fallen leaves and hurled it before us. It was then that I realised that what I had taken for a clearing ahead was a concealed patch of mud or swamp, for the branch lay on the moss-covered surface for but a moment and then was sucked down out of our sight.

'Good heavens, Holmes!' I exclaimed. 'If we had tried to cross that, we would have vanished without trace.'

'Most likely, but the sheen on the surface looked unnatural, even in this sparse moonlight. It was then that I remembered our previous experience.'

We retraced our steps, testing to ensure that the ground was firm until we found a place where a change of direction was possible. It was a wide detour, for the black and dangerous patch was spread over a greater area than we had at first thought. Moonlight faded and returned several times, and the denseness of the trees and the blackness proved formidable, but at last we left the forest behind and emerged into an open field. Before us was the stream, but narrower here and running with much less fury. The bridge was built higher than that we encountered earlier, resting on piled wooden trestles that had probably saved it from destruction. The rain had dwindled considerably, as we made our way up the gradual incline leading to the unfamiliar shape of Trentlemere Hall.

As we approached, I noticed that several downstairs rooms were lit, and one above. We found ourselves at the rear of the house and followed the terrace to the front, where a wide drive led away into the darkness to meet with the road. Presently we stood saturated before a wide iron-studded door, and Holmes knocked loudly. Footsteps echoed inside, getting louder, before the door creaked open.

A black-clad butler faced us, his expression solemn.

'Good evening, gentlemen,' he said gravely.

'I am Sherlock Holmes,' my friend replied, 'and this is my associate, Doctor Watson. We received a summons, in London, from Lord Trentlemere.'

The butler bowed his head. 'I am aware of that sir. Come in, please.'

We were shown into a pleasant drawing-room, with drawn curtains and a roaring fire, for which we were most thankful. The butler left us, taking our soaked hats and coats and assuring us that Lord Trentlemere would be with us shortly. As we warmed ourselves, Holmes pointed above the hearth at a heavily framed portrait.

'That is Lord Trentlemere,' he remarked, 'as I remember him. The likeness is excellent.'

A moment later we were joined by a young man of no more than twenty-five, who announced himself as Lord Trentlemere. I saw surprise cross Holmes' face.

'You were expecting my father, of course,' the young man said grimly. 'I regret to inform you of his death, early this morning. He is free of pain now and reunited with my mother.'

We expressed our condolences and for a while we talked, sitting in comfortable armchairs and drinking brandy, about Holmes' previous association with the Trentlemere estate.

'My father left instructions regarding the documents concerning the murderer of my sister,' the new Lord Trentlemere assured us during a lapse in the conversation. 'He was most explicit and satisfied that at last his years of research had not been in vain.'

'Do you know the nature of his evidence?' Holmes enquired.

'No, he did not confide that to me, but I can tell you that it has been examined by more than one group of solicitors, and that we have received assurances that it is valid and legally binding. My father said that you, Mr Holmes, would know how it should best be used.'

My friend nodded. 'The documents will be in the hands of Scotland Yard, on our return to London tomorrow.'

The young man smiled for the first time. 'Excellent. I can see that my father's trust was not misplaced. And now, gentlemen, there is a meal and rooms prepared for you. I expect you will wish to retire, after such an arduous journey.'

We rose and followed him out of the room. At the doorway I looked back at the portrait above the hearth, at the face of the man with the eye patch and drooping moustache. It was the face of the apparition that had warned us thrice this night, of calamities that lay ahead.

My friend glanced at me as if he had read my mind, and I wondered as to what his cold and logical mind had made of the strange events that had occurred during our journey. I knew I would learn nothing if I enquired, for in Holmes' view of life everything has a normal explanation.